WARNINGS FROM THE FUTURE

WARNINGS FROM THE FUTURE

STORIES

ETHAN CHATAGNIER

CINCINNATI 2018

Acre Books is made possible by the support of the Robert and Adele Schiff Foundation.

Printed in the United States of America
First printing

Designed by Barbara Neely Bourgoyne
Cover art: *Tight Loop* (cropped), painting by Skip Lawrence, reproduced with permission of the artist

Library of Congress Cataloging-in-Publication Data have been applied for.
ISBN-10 (pbk): 1-946724-03-3 / ISBN-13 (pbk): 978-1-946724-03-8
ISBN-10 (e-book): 1-946724-08-4 / ISBN-13 (e-book): 978-1-946724-08-3

The press is based at the University of Cincinnati, Department of English and Comparative Literature, McMicken Hall, Room 248, PO Box 210069, Cincinnati, OH, 45221–0069.
www.acre-books.com

Acre Books books may be purchased at a discount for educational use. For information please email business@acre-books.com.

For Laura

CONTENTS

WARNINGS FROM THE FUTURE

MIRACLE FRUIT

At 7 p.m., three-quarters of the recessed lights in the main office space are programmed to turn off. What's left is deemed bright enough for the custodial staff to do their work, but what I love, looking out through the interior window of my office, is that the glow of all the screensavers creates a faint aurora over the top of all the cubicle walls almost like that of a town at night hidden just beyond a ridge. I know it's just a silly image, but it gives me the sort of comfort I imagine God would feel looking at a snow-dusted Swiss village and allowing himself to forget the rest of the troubled world for a while. I stay late like this because it's the easiest time to handle the real, unbureaucratic work of thinking, planning, analyzing data, and so on. I also use the time to care for my *Synsepalum dulcificum,* misting it, trimming it, adding a little peat or some acidifying fertilizer, and for whatever reason these diversions provide me with the greatest clarity of thought I have all day. But I also like to stay late because, unlike at home, where my mother salts the air with her misery, the solitude here feels purposeful.

Tonight, I'm just finishing up a request for access to our latest acquisition. All the other project leads had their requests in last week, but I've been trying to get my wording, my logic, just right, in the hope that a strong argument will matter more than who was first to the starting line. But I know how it will go. Corn and soy will get the first crack at it. My wheat is beating yield estimates and making the company lots of money too—which I'm certain is why I haven't been talked to despite all the surveillance footage of me staying late to mommy a potted plant—but I know a lot of people are starting to see me as some sort of deluded prophet for continuing to believe that wheat has a place in the future.

In an office environment, logic can only do so much. I finish up my request and e-mail it to Meadows anyway.

Before I go, I plug in the humidifying contraption I've put together. *Synsepalum dulcificum* is from the jungles of west Africa, and the store-bought warm-water humidifier just wasn't enough, so I've connected a space heater to a litter box full of water, and wired in a little fan to circulate the humid air. Security has surely sent someone to investigate the strange apparatus, just to check, because anyone with a keycard for this facility has the know-how to make a bomb, even the technicians. Maybe even the custodians. But it doesn't take an engineering degree to see this setup is climate control for my shrub. It's been a lot perkier since I switched to this method. In the first half of the year it didn't bloom, but now it has eleven green buds on it, and all of them are starting to blush.

I like walking out to the deserted parking lot as well, no claustrophobia of cars, nobody yammering into a cell phone or blasting bad music, but tonight there is another car, a Camry with Avis stickers, and it's parked right next to mine. Leaning against it is a slender, copper-haired woman, wearing a fitted trench coat and kitten heels, who is definitely not from Nebraska.

"Can I ask you about Aeon, Dr. Schuyler?" she asks.

"Mother Jones?"

"New York Times."

Surprising. To someone like me, our Aeon acquisition is front page news, but most people would rather see pictures of a beheading or read a new brownie recipe. It's good that someone is paying attention, I think. But it's bad when a *New York Times* reporter ambushes you in the dark of an empty parking lot rather than contacting the corporate media office. It means this is just the slight visible outgrowth of a story already being tracked, of documents already being compiled and pieces put together. It means you are not just the person who picked up the phone; you were chosen. And why was I chosen? Because I am unmarried, because I have no children, because I own a small home outright and scrupulously save 60 percent of my income? All information readily available on a tax return. A few days of observation would reveal me to be the type to arrive first and leave last from work, the type to care for an elderly parent whose one remaining joy is complaining, and the type to carefully tend a backyard garden that I'm rarely home to enjoy. She is betting that I am the right combination of idealistic, lonely, and with little enough to lose that I might throw myself on the sword. She suspects that if confronted with a beautiful woman, I will want to speak to her, to please.

How close is she to right?

I tell her I can't help her. She hands me her business card anyway. Sharon Saxon—what a newspaper name. She counsels me not to bring the card back to this place.

When I get home, my mother tells me that all those dials on the washing machine do nothing. As with a baby toy, they are simply knobs that click. Cold and hot are the only true settings. The rest are illusions. This is just the latest in her litany of modern horrors. They're all she has these days. The chunky spaghetti sauce is the same as the nonchunky spaghetti sauce. The chunks in chunky peanut butter are microplastics. There are little bugs that look like dust. They look just like dust, but they are bugs. How can you tell, Mom? You can't. Last month she said her earwax smelled savory, like mushrooms with rosemary, like duck fat. No matter how good it smells, I told her, don't eat it.

"Hot and cold is all I need," I say, regarding the washing machine.

"Garage doors cause cancer. You should put yours on manual."

She's reached an age where there's no listening going on. She's all output. She prefers afghans now, though I offer her good quilts. Any chair she sits in instantly takes on the aura of a rocking chair, even the sofa. She's unhappier now than her own mother was at this age, and grandma had set the world record for unhappiness. I bring her a bowl of SpaghettiOs.

"I fed you kids vegetables."

"Ketchup and canned beans."

If I bring her zucchini, she'll say, "You know how I feel about zucchini." The same if I bring her kale or celery or butternut squash. She'll accept SpaghettiOs, mac and cheese, pork and beans—Depression food, pun intended—but she always offers that disclaimer: I fed you kids vegetables. The O's are made with rice flour now. Pretty much all pasta is, besides the luxury stuff. The sauce is sweetened with corn syrup. It's soybeans in pork and beans. The sauce is sweetened with corn syrup. The cheese powder in the mac and cheese is synthetically produced flavor crystallites. The milk you make it with is soy milk. The butter you mix in is hydrogenated corn oil with synthetically produced flavor crystallites.

"Why don't you go out to the garden?"

She does, though she's eaten only half of her bowl. She leaves it on the end table and heads out back. She fails to finish her meals, but even so her midsection is growing, though it seems to be airy and insubstantial, like rising bread dough. Is it a tumor, or a gland issue, or just following the Dada rules of the aging body after sixty? I don't know. Her health is a house of cards I don't want to blow on.

She's on the bench in the garden, making it seem like a rocking chair. Around her there's amaranth, leeks, chard, varicolored carrots, rare potatoes, the shoots of onion and garlic bulbs. There's a big bush of rosemary and a bit of thyme. Of the trees, the fuyu persimmon, ponderosa lemon, and alma fig are bearing fruit. I pluck a fuyu and take a bite. Its flesh is crisp, but the flavor, with traces of cinnamon, butter, and apple, is almost too delicate to exist.

"Why don't you have a fig for dessert?" I ask.

"You know how I feel about figs."

* * *

The Aeon seed bank was the last major seed bank in the world. It was in Annecy, France, not far across the border from the Geneva office of the United Nations, which, along with a dozen other foundations and entities, had subsidized its existence. But it was still a French property, still under the aegis of the French government, and with the spiral toward bankruptcy looming, they were vulnerable to Semillon making an offer they could hardly believe, let alone refuse. The papers and magazines that made a stink about the purchase comforted their readers with editorials arguing that transporting one and a half billion seeds in cold storage from eastern France to Nebraska was a logistical problem that would take at least five years to solve. What they didn't know was that Semillon had been working on the problem for eight years. Only a few conspiracy nuts were right about that part, though they destroyed any credibility with claims that Semillon had manufactured the French fiscal crisis to begin with.

On the first day of delivery, a line of semis stretches out of the campus and six miles down the highway. Exhaust hangs above the string of them like a heat mirage. Each carries a specially equipped refrigeration trailer, and at four docks the semis back in and robotic overhead cranes hook onto the trailers and guide them via a track system to a preprogrammed spot in the main refrigeration chamber, where they automatically sync with the facility's power system. No manual labor is required.

The protesters are late, showing up at 7:30 a.m., like me. The first trucks had queued up at 5:00. The procession is so slow, though, that the activists have no trouble lying down in front of an arbitrary truck and halting the line there. But a crowd of state police has been on the scene since 8:00, and the company has a cart full of coffee urns set out for them, and they haul the long-bearded activists out of the street pretty much as soon as their backs touch the ground. They leave unmolested the protesters standing on the shoulder with signs that read BIODIVERSITY IS PUBLIC PROPERTY or show poorly painted images of a globe locked in a jail cell.

I'm a little embarrassed to agree with them. But then, they are looking at the issue from only one angle. Our population is growing at an exponential rate, and crop yields at a linear rate. Already we have 9 billion people on a planet that can feed only 8 billion, while the ten-year projections have the population at 10 billion and food production at enough for 8.1 billion. And what happens when the food wars migrate to countries with nuclear arsenals?

There are two weeks of days like this, trucks creeping patiently along the highway, dejected protesters using one hand to hold picket signs and the other to check their phones. There are a lot of plant species in the world. Some of the seeds in this collection are from plants no longer extant, plants waiting to be revived, though mostly they wait in vain.

At the end of the second week of transit, Meadows calls me into his office and tells me I can have access to anything not earmarked by corn or soy, carte blanche, for one year. No need to file project memos and wait for approval, so long as I track what I use in the master database. It's an unprecedented level of access, an unprecedented cutting of red tape.

"Mind your deadlines, and don't take on too much."

"I've got a few big ideas."

"It all expires after a year," he reminds me.

"What happens in a year?"

I look at him. He looks at me. He's mastered the expression that says: I'm a scientist; I wish these weren't the realities we live with; I care. He's even better at it than I am.

"Pete," he says as I'm leaving. I stop in his doorframe. "You're doing important work."

"Everyone is, right?"

Our part of the campus is unadorned, utilitarian, but the Carthy Building, which faces the road, is designed to welcome corporate affiliates, board members, diplomats, and congressional representatives. It houses a tropical courtyard with one of the top-ranked koi ponds in the world. I don't know who ranks these things, but it is marvelous. Unreasonably calming. I spend the rest of the day there. I'm thinking about my most ambitious projects, narrowing them by those I can get off the ground within a year and have a reasonable chance of success. But mostly I'm thinking about nothing. Mostly I'm trying not to think about what happens in a year.

Sharon Saxon has been waiting for me in the parking lot every Tuesday night. She must be seeing signs that I'll crack, though I'm not sure what they are. I haven't stopped combing my hair. I'm still brushing my teeth. The Tuesday after my meeting with Meadows, I snap a berry off the *Synsepalum dulcificum*, perfectly red now, the shape of a grape tomato but a few shades darker. She's out there, all right. Her attire has mutated from what you'd wear to a client meeting to what you'd wear on a date. I imagine it's like a lockpick testing out a lock. A skirt now, respectable but shiny. Higher heels. A blouse coincidentally the same shade as my berry. Though how trustworthy is any coincidence when you're dealing with an investigative reporter? One of those silly jackets women wear that only go down as far as the ribs.

"Your father would tell you to wear a coat," I say.

"A gentleman would offer me his own."

I look down at the sleeves of my thin sweater. "Sorry. I'm from Vermont."

"I know." She manages the aura of a smoker without having a cigarette, a real miracle of science.

"I don't really want to know how much you know about me."

"Yes, you do. Just not all at once."

What I like is not her in her professional garb or her date clothes, not an inch more or an inch less of leg, not a certain amount of décolletage or the right heels. I like the process of it all, despite the constructions, despite the obvious ends fueling all these different means. What can I say? Who doesn't want to feel like a lock being picked?

"Any news?"

"No news," I say, as usual. But this time I hold out my closed fist, and she puts her hand under it, open. I place the red berry in the bowl of her palm.

"Eat this," I say. "Then eat a lemon."

On the way home I stop at the hardware store and buy ten feet of four-inch PVC and a few plastic totes.

Sharon Saxon is sitting in my garden early Wednesday morning when I head out with my watering can and trowel. She's holed up in the corner of my park bench, wearing the kind of sweats that fancy people jog in, and she lights up when she sees me. She's waiting for a *good morning* or something, but I've decided to play it coy. Coy is as close to charming as a plant geneticist can get.

"It took me about three hours to convince myself you weren't trying to poison me."

"You're here, aren't you?"

"And I kept thinking it was some kind of code. But what is this berry, what's the lemon supposed to mean?"

"Did you try it?"

"Yeah, I finally went out and bought a bag of fucking lemons. This is incredible, Pete. Did you make it?"

I laugh. "The climate of west Africa made it, and a thousand individual pressures. Though it's anyone's guess as to why it's a selected-for trait. Nothing too useful, or it would be more common. *Synsepalum dulcificum*. They call it the miracle fruit."

"Have you thought of selling this to New York chefs? They'd pay a fortune."

"Don't tell me you're not familiar with the pleasure of keeping a secret."

My mother shuffles out the back door with a bowl of Frosted Flakes, leaving the screen open behind her. She's up two hours earlier than usual. Either Sharon woke her hopping the fence, or she sensed my happiness and has emerged to destroy it. She sits down on the other corner of the bench while I go on watering.

"There's a great beauty in the amazing diversity of plant life. Not just in the jungles, but in a place like this. It was never just grass, despite what the movies show. And the plainsmen who grazed it to death were not immune to its beauty. They just had families to feed."

"I sense a point emerging."

"So, one way of looking at it is that I have an overly generous definition of family."

All the while, we can hear my mother crunching her cereal. She watches Sharon Saxon with as much of a twinkle in her eyes as I do.

"Would you like a persimmon, Mom?"

"That sounds delightful," she says.

I feel it too, Mother. I didn't know you could.

"Sharon?"

"Any more magic fruits?"

"Miracle. And only at the office."

"Then sure, a persimmon."

We all take bites and soak up the flavor slowly. I wait for my mother to say something like "Toothpaste is made of recycled taxidermy," but apparently she doesn't want to offer her insights to the larger world.

"So what is the other way of looking at it?" Sharon asks.

"Just don't paint me as some kind of Mengele, okay?"

"What do you have?"

I tell her I have nothing but a scent on the wind. Then I suggest that she keep her hotel reservation open.

Fall gives way to winter, though the work we do makes the seasonal shift increasingly less relevant.

Meanwhile, I snoop around the work intranet. I lack the skill to avoid leaving digital footprints, but I buy myself some time by wearing Meadows's shoes. The oscillating cameras in his corridor are surprisingly easy to time. He doesn't lock his office and he doesn't log out of his computer and he doesn't delete his e-mail. And how much did the company pay for its cybersecurity training? I want to write the figure on a Post-it and leave it on his monitor.

The memo isn't hard to find. I knew the gist from that patented look-between-scientists he offered when he gave me my deadline. But since I have an idea what the *New York Times* would tell me to do with my gist, I need something more detailed. And there it is: an e-mail that says that the security risks of holding on to the bank outweigh its value as an asset; that says it would be more detrimental *to the company* [emphasis mine] if the bounty of these seeds escaped containment than if the smallpox virus did; that recommends incineration. Attached is a suggested schedule for the incinerations: flowers, vines, and other non-fruiting plants first. Then non-orchard trees. Then fruit and nut trees. Then bulbs and vegetables. Last, grasses and grains.

First they came for the Socialists, et cetera, et cetera.

Meanwhile, every day I'm bringing home a bucket of ammonium nitrate fertilizer and carting it down to my workshop in the basement. They track how much of this stuff people buy at hardware stores and nurseries. Not at the company.

Meanwhile, my mother has kept asking about Sharon Saxon, and what can I say, I've created a lie that keeps the two of us happy. Sharon thinks she might extend her stay even after she finishes her story. She's been taking me out to dinners to conduct interviews, but we often get lost in discussions irrelevant to Semillon, conversations about nature and history and the unforgiving beauty of selection, both natural and artificial. My mother still insists that television technology has always been flat-screen, that they built a big empty space inside the old blocky TVs because they weren't sure how people would react, but she tells me over a plate of wild rice and home-cooked vegetables.

In truth, Sharon has been waiting for me Tuesdays, as always, and I've given her little bits of information, but mostly seeds. Every Tuesday, a new batch. *Albuca spiralis. Randia ruiziana. Musa acuminata*. I don't know that she'll plant them. I don't know that she can keep them alive if she does. I just know that they're out. Two seeds in my hand become two seeds in her hand.

So this is what it's come to? Schuyler's List?

Imagine a kid setting off his first firecracker, only to learn that the sound of the blast is less impressive than the pop when he opens a shaken soda can. The word itself, *blast,* becomes instantly ridiculous. There you have the blast that failed to shake the globe, or even the little old Cornhusker State, when the news broke that Semillon Incorporated planned to destroy the world's greatest repository of biodiversity. The *New York Times*: page 4. Another round of bush-bearded protesters lying down in front of basic delivery trucks, and some op-eds aimed at the already converted. Still, I go into work prepared to be served with papers or taken into custody or led by security down some ill-lit hallway, never to return. Dust Meadows's keyboard for fingerprints and they've got me. Ask around among the custodians and they've probably got me. Instead, Meadows is gone, and there's a meeting in which they caution us to neither initiate nor accept contact with him pursuant to the settling of a legal action. In fact, they say, if anyone sees him, walk straight out of the room, army-crawl beneath the windows, and call security from the first phone you see.

Sorry, bro. You never should have gone into administration.

The suit brought against Semillon is dropped after initial hearings. No one has standing to sue, the judge says. No individual can claim harm. In his twelve-page decision, the judge writes that he is not happy having to make this ruling. He sympathizes with the people saying the incineration would be a crime against humanity. No, he writes, it is a crime against something else. A crime, probably, against something worse, but something unfortunately not protected by the law. It seems logical. He's doing his job. I'm not really doing mine anymore. Wheat and rice are being planted over by the hectare anyway. Once they're gone, corn and soy can duke it out for who has better numbers. There can be only one.

Sorry, wheat. You should have been more calorific.

Snow in the parking lot, and Sharon standing tall in it, like a candle, asking if I can find any documents relating to Semillon's involvement in the French recession. She knows that would be out of my division even if it were more than a rumor. Even asking shows her desperation. She appears harried now, like a wife. It's a much more beautiful look, hair frizzed, eyes bagged, like a person who exists in the world.

I tell her I'll find what I can. I know what that will be.

Security has clamped down since the leak. Cameras have been added to cover blind spots. IT has been given the authority to publicly yell at people with stupid passwords. The only way for me to search around is with my own login information, and that only gets me into a space with very well-defined fences. I'm likely to have only one shot at testing those boundaries, and I'm not ready to take it yet. What does it matter? I keep wondering. The memo I gave Sharon *was* the smoking gun. Unless Semillon is planning to toss some babies into the incinerator with the seeds, no one is going to care. Given the quandaries of overpopulation, some might not even balk at that. Crop yields—we all bow to that god now.

But I've told her I am waiting for my opportunity. Still doing what? Working up the nerve; working in my basement; cultivating fantasies; ferrying plants across the Styx, bearing them back ceaselessly against the flow of time.

Brugmansia arborea. Rafflesia arnoldii. Strongylodon macrobotrys.

Sharon. Harper. Saxon.

Seeds passing from my hand to hers, little things, dried and hard and unassuming, displaying no pomp for all the information they contain. *Phoenix dactylifera.* The Judean date palm, extinct for six hundred years, was resurrected from a two-thousand-year-old seed lost in a jar. This is no more than the pit of a date, the thing you spit out when you eat one.

I tell Sharon she'll have to come to my house to get what I've found. I tell her she doesn't have to Batman into the garden, but she does anyway. It's warm again, a morning in April during which there's a whole different crop of fruit and vegetables. Only the ponderosa lemons are the same. Oh, tired but hopeful eyes. Is there a more heartbreaking sight?

I smile a smile I've been saving up for her. I unclasp my fist in front of her, my big reveal: two red berries just longer than olives. We chew the pulp away from the pits and swirl it around in our mouths to coat as much of the surface as we can. It tastes like almost nothing. The secret, I tell her, is a glycoprotein, uncreatively named miraculin, which binds to the taste buds and blocks bitter and sour compounds. The properties, of course, were known long before the mechanism.

By the time I've finished my pedantry, it's taken effect. We set upon the lemon tree. We bite into them without peeling them. The insides taste like lemonade. The white pith tastes like meringue. We eat whole lemons this way, not bothering to spit out the seeds. I yank other things out of the garden: arugula, which now tastes like some kind of crazy herb sorbet; rhubarb like raspberry jam; radishes like sweetened ice. But we go back to the lemon tree. It seems to be what this was made for—ambrosia, jellied light bulbs. The miracle doesn't keep our bellies from feeling full, from growing hot with acid, but we keep going.

The miraculin lasts about thirty minutes. We start to pucker as the lemons turn back into lemons. We look at each other and laugh, but it's hard to keep up the merriment as we feel our teeth ache, our throats burn, our stomachs roil, and the truth that we've just gorged on raw lemons becomes once again unavoidable. I tell her I want a favor before I give her the document I've found. I tell her my mother's grown fond of her, that she doesn't get out much. I ask her to drive my mother around town for half an hour, showing her whatever she wants to see. When I go inside, my mother is already up making coffee and sparing me her theory that it was all ground at the same time in one great coffee bean holocaust. I let her know about Sharon taking her out for a spin.

"Oh," she says, brightening. "Then I should put on something more presentable."

She comes out of her room wearing slightly moth-holed but still bright pastels from a friendlier decade. I tell her she looks nice.

Once they've gone, I head down to the basement. It's a simple enough calculation, scaling the reactants down and filling the empty space in the pipe with chalk. I'd made it big enough to destroy half of the refrigeration chamber at the seed bank. I thought of putting it in an intermodal container and driving a big rig up to the loading docks, letting the routing system deliver it. But of course there's no way to get it through security, and there's no point. What good is a bomb for saving something from destruction? We scientists with our strange meditative acts. Too fancy for yoga or sudoku. But this one doesn't have to go to waste. I think I've got the right amount to just destroy my own basement. The living room and kitchen, if my decimal points are off. The blast will certainly be small enough to spare the garden, though I have little hope that anyone will tend it.

I write out the document on a piece of stationery and place it like a bookmark in chapter six of Genesis in my mother's Bible. I've never been religious, but I do believe in parables. I place the book on the park bench out back. It is not the document she's hoping for. It simply reads *Sorry. There is nothing to be done.* I leave it next to a little brown bag containing the eight remaining miracle berries. I consider writing out the rest of what follows, but decide not to be one of those men who needs to inflict his pain upon the world.

But if I were, here is what I would write. The problem all along has been with trying to see myself as the savior in this parable, or at least a Good Samaritan. But my role is much smaller than that, much plainer. I've realized I'm here simply to update an old verse for a modern age:

God saw evil in the hearts of men. He repented of having made them. God planned to flood the earth, but he had some reservations. He had Noah build an ark. Noah built according to God's specifications, including the coating of pitch, and he ushered into it all the animals of the world—fliers, walkers, creepers, and so on—and he secured them in their cells. Then the great flood came and drowned the earth, but the ark was buoyed safely up. It floated on the water a while, above the obliterated world. Long enough for Noah to take some comfort in the work he'd done. Then, after a time, whether because God willed it, or because he didn't care enough to stop it—and let the angels debate over whether it's a meaningful difference—the ark caught fire. The ark sank.

SMALLER TRAGEDIES

In the foreground of the photograph, a boy stands on the double yellow line of a four-lane highway. He could be nine years old, but it is difficult to tell. His posture makes him seem older, erect and still, with one arm hanging loosely by his side and the other outstretched toward the viewer. His expression makes him seem much younger: his eyes averted, the pupils in the far left corners, and his mouth wide open in the uncomprehending anguish of a toddler, conveying surprise as much as pain, exposed to a new and raw angle on the world. He is sharpened by the depth of focus, but the background is still sharp enough to make out the details. Cars, at least eight, mashed together, no longer in their sleek and recognizable shapes, just different colors of clay in roughly car-shaped blocks. There is a huge produce truck as well, turned over on its side, and the ground behind the boy is carpeted with strawberries.

Alice woke Carmen with Carmen's camera bag already packed, and only enough underwear, Alice told her, for three days. The Big One had hit at 6:04 a.m. with an epicenter near Daly City, and the faint echoes of it could be felt all the way down in Santa Ana. The vibrations weren't strong enough to wake anyone so far south, but Alice had been up, and she turned on the news expecting to hear about a 2-point-something originating in La Brea. As soon as she'd seen footage of the tunnel, she knew. Alice wouldn't kiss Carmen goodbye, but woke Dean so that he could. Dean marched out in his footies for a perfunctory smooch, rubbing crusts out of his eyes. He'd go back to bed for another hour or two. He knew the drill. It was routine these days. Driving toward disaster had become the way of Carmen's life. She was home now, fulfilling that wrung promise to the two of them to stay out of war zones and Kevlar, and smaller tragedies would have to do.

Years before the quake hit San Francisco, she'd learned to shun the picturesque, so she skipped the coastal highways and headed north on the 99, a curveless, ratty vein through the heart of the state, dotted with produce stands and worn trailers and low, peeling motels that might or might not have been abandoned. She preferred it to the 101 through Paso Robles, with its beautiful tree-broccolied hills and stands of eucalyptus, and then dark-earthed rows of garlic and strawberries as you passed through Gilroy. Highway 1 was among the most scenic roads in the world, the waves polishing great boulders sticking up like thumbs from the foamy California surf, cliffsides green with flora, and old arching bridges over the tributaries that fed the Pacific. It wasn't that she didn't love beauty. Of course she loved beauty. Everyone loved beauty. It was a bit obvious, though, wasn't it?

It took a certain perspective to see any in the Grapevine this time of year. Even in the purple dawn the peaks of the Tehachapis were dull tan mounds, so like massive swept piles of dust it was difficult to imagine any rock inside them, and they were freckled only by low creeping brush that offered no suggestion that a man or even a field mouse could take nourishment from it. But as she rounded the last bend and came upon the long straight grade that descended into the San Joaquin Valley, she saw the whole of it filled with fog like a bowl of dirty cotton. As the mountains dropped away behind her and it was just her and the road, plummeting into it, she thought of the more familiar image of lowering through a cloud bank on an airplane descent, and was stupidly surprised not to feel any turbulence as she plunged through.

She felt a thrill as the fog surrounded the car, no bumps, no force pushing back at her, none of the resistance the bank of dull white seemed to suggest from outside. She loved the way it dematerialized in front of her as if opening a secret pathway, and without thinking she pressed her foot down a little more on the gas pedal. Without landmarks to gauge her speed, she'd have thought that the fog would have made everything seem slower, but instead it felt like the most furious racing. She looked at her speedometer, the same 70 mph. Her breakfast lurched in her stomach and the skin of her face cooled as she asked herself how long would it take her to use up her fifty feet of visibility going that speed? How many feet would it take to stop the jeep? She pulled to the shoulder, slamming her foot to the brake, and the jeep rocked violently as a big rig she hadn't seen behind her shot by, erupting with a foghorn so loud the sound seemed to originate within her own head. She laid her head down on the top of the steering wheel and heard a crunch at the same time she felt prongs dig into the bridge of her nose. Her sunglasses: she'd forgotten she was wearing them. She took them off, and the fog—bright and pearly—seemed lit from within.

This is what she remembers, what she tries to remember first, what she tries to keep her mind on later, when she looks at the photo that's framed on the wall of her home office. It's a simple frame, taking no attention away from its subject. She'd originally hung it above the mantle, and Alice had made her take it down. *You want our guests to look at this? You want our friends to be in discomfort every moment they are in our house? Do you want Dean to grow up under this?* She'd agreed to move it, and Alice had replaced it with a family portrait Carmen had taken with a timer. That was the problem with war photography, and with the disaster-chasing it had turned into here at home: trying to show people things they preferred not to see. No, that was only one of the problems, for Carmen herself, even years later, was filled with conflict when looking at the photo.

The fog was so complete that the jeep itself seemed not to exist. Every so often she opened her door to see the yellow median dashes crawl by and confirm she was still on the right side of the road. If Alice knew the type of soup Carmen was driving in, she'd settle for nothing less than Carmen reversing time to avoid having left LA in the first place. They'd argued enough about Carmen's work, about her running to places others were running from. That was what Alice had fallen in love with, though she wouldn't admit it now—the life Alice had admired before being shackled to it. Dean had changed everything for Alice; for Carmen, Dean had changed some things. Without Dean toddling around in her memory, she wouldn't have been crawling along at ten miles an hour, no matter the visibility. But she could never *not go*.

She didn't know what towns she was between when the fog thinned out suddenly. After a moment she could see the wind funneling it into a deep river bed. Gusts of the thick mist seemed to be not blown but sucked into the channel as if in one ceaseless inhale. The river of fog ran east, which is to say backwards, against instinct. The flares caught her eye a moment too late as the wreck ahead impressed its meaning on her consciousness in one powerful stamp. She swung the wheel to the right and flew across the shoulder and onto the steep embankment. Tire treads bit at the loose dirt, and she slid for several feet before they grabbed and halted the jeep.

She left it there, out of the way of the road, unbuckling her camera bag from the passenger seat and slinging it over her shoulder. She grabbed a first aid kit from the glove box and slid it into the mesh pouch of the camera bag. While she charged up the embankment, she got her camera strap around her neck and affixed a lens, outlining the situation as best she could: no lights or sirens, no aid yet; flares, at least on this side of the wreck. She called 911 and told them about the pileup. Where was it? "Between Bakersfield and

Fresno," she said. "I don't fucking know." As she got level with the bridge the wreck was on the far side of, she saw a scattering of people against the guardrail, heads in hands, in postures of mourning. There were doubtless some people imprisoned or crushed in those accordioned cars. A man leaned against his smashed Corolla, uselessly banging on its roof. She knew the red cover on the ground could not be blood, must have been tomatoes or cherries or berries, but they made for a grisly sight.

She was framing shots in her mind at the same time she was doing a medical triage. It would help no one to bang on the side of the car with that man, but she could see the angle from which it would make a compelling image. The survivors against the guardrail could use a neuro check that she was marginally equipped to perform, but it wouldn't do any good until ambulances arrived anyway. There were a thousand ways she could help, of course. She could find things. The dictum in foreign countries was to be strictly hands off: there were soldiers for soldiering and medics for medicine. That policy was harder to maintain on the domestic front.

As she walked into the scene, she felt the crimson bursting of the strawberries beneath her feet. She took several shots of the people hunched over in front of the guardrail, between the rough wet asphalt below them and the backdrop of fog swirling down into the basin. She took some of the man banging on the car, cautiously out of his sightlines at first, in case he was demented enough to attack her, but then closer, toward the shot she really wanted. His face snapped up at her, but it was broken by grief, and he went back to beating the car. She retreated from him, and that was when she saw the boy.

He had walked around the far edge of the produce truck from the other side of the wreck, and was approaching her. He was not screaming, but he was not swaying his arms as he walked either. A thin line of dried blood went from his hair past his ear and down his neck. There is something about a person who is in true need of help, something that creates a beacon, even if they say nothing.

The story she tells herself—that she saw the boy and took the picture by instinct before she even thought about it. It sounds so natural and true that sometimes she almost forgets it didn't happen that way. But she did have that thought: this will make a great photograph. She put the box to her eye to snap it, just a single exposure that imprinted itself in her memory immediately. Sometimes you didn't know what you had until you saw it in the darkroom, but this was not one of those times. She took it and then rushed to help: throwing her windbreaker around him, picking him up, talking to him, and taking him over to the group by the guardrail.

She took it knowing she would feel guilty. Those were the taxes of the job. What was war photography but choosing the ghosts that would haunt you? She is stuck too with remembering wanting to be in a darkroom more than wanting to help the dumbstruck victims, given what she had in her film compartment. Already the image was a conduit to Dean, who was sleeping placidly in his bed a hundred miles south. Dean was three or four years younger, but it was close enough for that thing to happen, the thing that happens to every parent, the thing by which any suffering child looks at you with the eyes of your own child. She'll remember too trying to wipe sweat from her forehead afterward and realizing she was still wearing the cowboy hat she'd been driving in. The poor boy must have felt he'd been visited by a tourist.

How many times has she wondered, standing in front of the photograph, whether she had taken something from the boy? A part of her thought she had stolen every expression from him except the one in the picture. But that was just a photographer's vanity. Even the word *capture* was a photographer's vanity. You created a duplicate of one instant, and then the instant went on. The ambulances and fire trucks arrived. An EMT took the boy. Others hovered their fingers in front of the eyes of the victims on the shoulder. They used machines to pry the doors off the Corolla and remove part of the bewildered man's wife. Carmen had left after that, but she knew that the tow trucks would be next, peeling the cars apart and carting them two at time to some mechanic's yard in a nearby town where they'd wait on an insurance assessment. She didn't know how they'd handle the big rig and its trailer. It would likely take a few tow trucks working together to get it righted. And what would they do with the strawberries? Would they send a street sweeper to clean them up, or leave them to the slower fate of the birds?

Either way, systems were already in action erasing the whole scene.

War was the same. It buried the memory of itself as it went. That's why recording it was important. But disasters and accidents? There was no horror of human conflict to illuminate, no peace to protect. It could be argued that the sum of the good this photograph could do was as a PSA: Be Careful Driving in the Fog. One could argue as well for the importance of witness. This accident that deconstructed the lives of thirteen people happened on a day that had made their suffering quotidian. Without a record, the fact of the wreck would simply diffuse into the higher buzz of the quake's aftermath. And yet standing there, or even looking at the picture, the greater tragedy in the Bay Area was wholly separate for her, abstract and irreconcilable.

Carmen had been listening to the radio on the drive. The retrofitting of the bridges and buildings in San Francisco had done its job, but a section of the north bore of the Caldecott Tunnel had caved in, potentially on some early morning commuters, and a twelve-story brick building in downtown Oakland had collapsed. The reporters hadn't yet ascertained whether the structure was commercial or residential, but with their voices raw they hoped that it was commercial, as a commercial building would be nearly empty at 6 a.m., while a residential one—they didn't finish their sentences. The woman they'd pull out of the rubble two days later, who would go on to write a memoir and do the morning-show circuit, had been trapped beneath the building at the same time that boy had wandered out of the wreckage, and yet in those moments the two mattered nothing to one another.

Witness: did the boy want this moment in his life to be seen, documented? Did anyone but Carmen want to witness it?

Alice would not look at the picture. She barely came into the office after it went up, not because she didn't care about the boy but because she cared too much. It was in a museum as well, where tourists could stand in front of it, feel a whiff of sympathy, then move on to a whiff of the next thing.

You took something that stuck with you. You hoped it stuck with other people. You could tell a good photograph when looking at it felt like trying to find a key locked inside the box that the key opens. The low wisps of fog mimicking smoke, the strawberries mimicking blood. They didn't mean anything. They didn't mean nothing either.

Back in the jeep, she imagined driving up to the 580 and taking it west to I-80, telling herself that whatever picture most defined the earthquake would be not only in the *New York Times* and on the *Today* show but in history books and stock reels for the rest of time. It was a sales pitch to herself. She remembered taking I-80 east all the way from San Francisco to New York after she'd graduated college, documenting refugee communities along the way. And now she felt with a desire that was primal, almost sexual, an impulse to take her shameful, exhilarated, independent self across the country once more.

But when she thought of the image that she'd taken—when she developed it she'd find her recollection of it was almost perfect—there was the boy's suffering staring out at her with Dean's eyes, and it was undeniable that she existed tied to others. It felt like a kind of defeat. She turned around and took the 99 back to Los Angeles.

When she came into the city she went straight to the darkroom co-op. She couldn't recall the last time she'd been so impatient waiting for negatives to develop, or for a print in its developer bath. She made a 24×36, though larger ones would come later. For the moment she wanted something she could hold with her arms angled out, the boy close enough to her size that he could look her in the eyes. She held him awhile like that, not conversing.

At home, Alice and Dean were still in their pajamas, sitting next to each other on the couch. Alice was working on her laptop while Dean recited a library book from memory. Later in life, when she wanted to remember the two of them, she remembered this afternoon, coming in on them so innocent and undisturbed.

"What are you doing back?" Alice asked. Dean glanced up from his book and went back to reading it.

"I got what I needed."

Seeing the skepticism on Alice's face, she put on a movie for Dean and poured two glasses of the Bordeaux they'd opened last night—hard to believe they'd been home having a normal dinner less than a day ago—and the two of them sat together at the kitchen table. It was the sort of conversation that should happen as the night stretches late, their faint doubles reflected in the window glass, but here they were having it in the midafternoon, with daylight on the patio ferns and the kitchen still smelling like coffee as they drank their leftover wine. She told Alice about the fog, omitting her near miss with the semi, and about coming upon the accident, how instinct guided her as she documented the scene. And then about the boy, how he walked out of the wreck toward her, how his blankness was a scream. She told Alice too about the guilt she felt when she took the picture, which she usually would not have shared. It was the sharing that came naturally to early dates and first years, but was so rare now, in the marriage years, with pleasantness overwhelming everything.

Then Carmen showed her the photograph, and was once again so entranced by the image that she paid no attention to Alice's response. By the time Carmen looked over, Alice was looking away. Knowing she was being watched, Alice looked at the photo again, and the discomfort that washed over her was as obvious as if she were being forced to look at a sucking chest wound or a gnarly infection. Such different responses to the same thing, like something from an absurdist play. This is a fracture, Carmen thought. Though such fractures could be necessary to a relationship, the way fire is to a forest.

Within a few days the photo was matted and framed. Then it went on the mantel, briefly, before it was banished to the office. It watched over the rest of her life. Even when she was in her late middle years, when she and Alice were divorced and Alice had remarried, when Dean was off in college deciding whether he still liked them, the picture added new threads to the web of memories strung to it. And so the picture began to mean many things that were not presented by its image. Take it as an artifact unhitched from time, and see the many Carmens at many ages, in many circumstances, many moods, gazing into it. It teaches her this now: moments of your life can be tethered to one another. In looking at the photograph, she saw Dean when he was five, like when she took the photo, and as he was when he was nine and looked so much like the boy in the picture that her fears of him maimed or terrified were brought to life, and she saw herself walking out of the office to find him a teenager eating a bowl of cereal in the breakfast nook, walking out of the office to see him as an undergraduate—poorly shaven, electrically sullen, captivating—and she saw that strange boy as he was in a moment of suffering that had long passed, and she saw all the suffering of the world, and she saw herself able to detach from it.

The night she came home with the photo, she'd hugged Dean with a love fueled by the shame of not helping a boy like him. She held him so long he grew bored with the hug. The year he was three he'd climbed into her lap every time they hugged, and held the embrace until she stood up. He was still a sweet boy, so sweet that she worried about him, but his eyes had an adult tiredness to them sometimes. He'd looked like he could use some coffee. Only five, but already burnt a little more each year by the wildness of the world.

When Carmen showed him the image the next morning, he took half a step backward but did not look away as Alice had. He stared at it with such a raw concern that Carmen thought he might speak to it, but the questions he asked were practical in nature: *Where were the boy's parents? Did the police and the ambulances come? Were* you *in the crash? Where would that boy go?*

RETROGRADE MOUNTAIN TIME

Do voices age? I don't mean the thickening of puberty or the weak wind of old age, but within one phase of a man's life—say, from thirty-four to forty-three? I was asking myself this question as I quietly stepped down the hallway past the girls' rooms, taking a call in the dark from a Tahoe area code, which meant someone from the past. In the bedroom, it was a voice whose familiarity could not be matched to memory. In the hallway I was fairly certain it belonged to my brother Rick, though the voice was babbling, and Rick was not one to babble. In the kitchen, turning on the little light under the microwave that usually only Denise used, that she sometimes forgot to turn off when we closed up the house for bed, I was sure—both because I'd heard enough that I could filter out what I thought was a little extra graveliness—a little more suggestion of beef or Skoal—to turn it into the voice I used to know, and because now he was saying, *It's Shasta, Bill. It's Shasta.* Shasta was my niece. Shasta was his daughter.

Through his hysterics I gathered she'd been stabbed in a bar and he was rushing her to Barton Memorial down in South Lake. As soon as he said this, it was like I was watching a live feed. I knew those roads so well I could see his truck weaving down them, his headlights making the trunks of the conifers real in the night. The lake just made an empty blackness at this hour, except where the lights of Reno glimmered off the far side of it like a smear of Impressionist paint. I knew exactly how fast you could take those turns without veering across the narrow shoulder and tumbling down the mountain into the lake, though this was more a memory of a knowledge than a knowledge in earnest. I could see his truck, the shade of matte grape blue that could only be produced by age, its brake lights flashing red when he felt he'd hit a turn too fast. He likely had a new truck by now, but what could I see other than what I knew? I saw my brother as he was nine years ago. Had he shaved his beard in the interim, or trimmed it, or done anything to demonstrate that he, rather than it, was in charge?

I'd seen Shasta six years earlier at her eighth-grade graduation. She was fourteen, and I still imagined her that way, which managed not to chafe my mental image of the ride too much, because her breasts and hips were already exploding at a rate any father of daughters could only describe as dangerous. My own girls were developing more patiently, and into more refined silhouettes, and I've never been able to rid myself of the silly notion that choices I'd made had influenced this: the mortgage, the life insurance, the college funds. But buttoned-up uncles have a special affection for their wild-hearted nieces, just as wild-hearted uncles have a soft spot for their honor-roll nieces. I'd felt I could talk to Shasta as an adult. She had the bearing of one; she spoke to me as if she were one, as if her education in all things, abbreviated though it might be, was completed. I had expected to hear about some boy with a skateboard or a guitar or hair in his eyes. Instead she told me that she wasn't a mountain girl. She wouldn't do what her dad had done, wouldn't stay. She was a beach girl, she said, and she would be a beach woman once she had her diploma.

"You can stay with us in Sacramento," I said. "Still a ways from the beach, but close enough to the Delta."

She scoffed. "I'm talking Santa Cruz, Santa Barbara."

"Santa something."

"Exactly."

She didn't realize that in her choker, in her too-tight t-shirt and heavy eyeliner and sturdy shoes, she looked like the very picture of a mountain girl, and that by claiming to be destined for the beach, she was only cleaving tighter to norms of the girls who stayed. She'd spoken her intention so confidently I believed her in the moment, though driving back down into the valley, I knew better. If I had thought of her in the past few years, I would have been able to predict she'd spend her Saturday nights in one of those washout bars that served anyone over eighteen. But I would not have predicted any bloodshed.

"What happened?" I asked Rick.

"I'm applying pressure. What else should I do?"

"Is the knife still in the wound?"

"No."

"Do you think it might have hit a major organ?"

"Can you listen, Bill? It's four or five slices, high up on her thighs."

"Jesus Christ," I said. "Where was he trying to stab her?"

He let silence be his answer, the first moment of quiet since I'd picked up the phone. For a moment I was back at the kitchen table, my eyes fixed to the microwave in a way I hadn't realized, taking in the little circle of light, the oven's control console, and the ceramic cooktop that bounced some extra light back up to the ceiling, where it nested, light blue, in the recesses of the kitchen's main lights.

"How do I know if he got the femoral?"

"Is she still alive?" I asked. "Then he didn't get the femoral."

Talking down to him was the best way to ease his worry. I won't say it didn't also feel good, won't say I didn't want him to be thinking that his daughter would have been better off if it were me in the cab with her instead of him, that I had the skills to properly assess the wounds, that if I had concerns about her bleeding out on the drive I could have put in some emergency sutures with the fishing line in his tackle box and some sterile alcohol. In truth, so long as no major arteries were cut and they were doing a decent job applying pressure, I was more concerned about her going septic from whatever might have been on the blade, whatever might be on the towels or rags that were handy in Rick's truck. Doubtless he knew without asking that my own daughters were sleeping soundly in their beds, that if they'd stayed up past ten at all it would be to read surreptitiously under the covers, that even when they reached Shasta's age there was no way they'd spend their Saturday nights downing piss beer at bars populated by middle-aged men trying to drink enough to crack themselves open.

I heard Shasta moan, long and mournfully, and there they were again, my brother from nine years ago, my niece from six years ago, winding along the side of the mountains with white towels in her lap, a red penumbra spreading across them, the thighs of her jeans already saturated with blood, looking like something from a horror film. I saw her elbow thrown across her eyes like someone trying to nap on an airplane, less because of any physical wounds than to avoid interacting with her father. I saw the part of her face you see beneath a superhero's mask, her jaw set with emotion, glazed with tears, white from the loss of blood.

"How's her color?"

"Pale."

"Gray at all? Blue?"

"Just pale."

"That's good."

He was at least half an hour from the hospital. There was not much else I could tell him. The situation sounded as stable as it could be for an injured person riding through the dark in a dirty pickup. But he didn't hang up, so neither did I.

Rick had taken a swing at me at a family barbecue over a matter of probate. When our father died, the whole of his estate was his cabin in Tahoe, which had been our vacation home before the divorce and his only home in the years after. Rick had wanted to take over the house, but of the hundred and fifty thousand he needed to buy me out, he had about five.

Our mother, who had lost the Sacramento house after a banker boyfriend talked her into a host of ill-considered investments, was working as a waitress in Truckee and getting older. She could move out of her apartment, and she and Rick could share the house. It would be good for the family. Good for the family mattered to me, but I still had my loans from physician's assistant school, and Denise and I were still upside-down on our mortgage. We hadn't even started our 529 plans for the girls. Gifting that kind of equity was untenable. I thought it a breach for him to even ask, so it was perhaps in an ungenerous tone that I suggested the two of them go in on an apartment together.

That's when he took his swing, and yes, it did connect.

After that, I sent my lawyer to talk to him and his. He never apologized. My mother considered my failure to give them half a house miserly, so I lost her in the deal, too. She was a type you see often enough in movies, a lifetime of stints as a diner waitress and bartender, interrupted only by marriages to more successful men. She was pretty in a blunt way that hadn't aged well, turning her into one of those square-jawed old ladies that made me think of extras in spaghetti westerns.

Shasta's graduation party had been at my mother's apartment complex, hot dogs in the park-style grill boxes poking up around a pool whose unnatural turquoise color screamed of some kind of carcinogenic additive. A few families were in the pool, but no one from our group. We all stood dopily on the grass in the June heat. There was no mixing between the two populations of our party—Shasta's friends and my mother's. I'd come to see Shasta, knowing Rick was off in Goose Lake near the Oregon border seeing about a used boat. I didn't want to see her tumble into a family rift she'd played no part in creating. My mother made a few crossings to offer the girls Ruffles from a melamine bowl, but she knew where her tribe was. I was stuck between the two. My mother didn't come talk to me, and I didn't go talk to her. Neither did I have any desire to hover around a group of six teenagers. Shasta finally resolved my dilemma by deserting her friends to talk with me awhile. She held her bottled Coke the way men held beer bottles at patio parties, with a thumb and three fingers, nonchalant, elbow bent to keep it at rib height, as if it were a microphone she might soon need to speak into. She was more practiced with the real thing, I suspected, from parties at which her grandmother wasn't lurking. And the way she pulled up next to me, rather than facing me, so that we were looking out together at the kids half-submerged in the industrial-solvent-colored pool, made me worry she might light up a cigarette.

"How's Denise?" she asked.

The way she posed this simple question, as if asking were a dry joke, contained a fully formed critique of my wife: that she was too limited in her worldviews, that she was simple in her attempts to find balance and meaning through inspirational pictures and motivational quotes, that she did not know how to be a real person. Shasta, even in her elementary school years, had not bought into the pleasant and extremely mommish way Denise tried to lead her and the girls through activities. She perhaps thought there was something dishonest about that kind of acting, that it was concealing a void, that it was a sheet of wrapping paper over no gift. It was certainly not an act that Rick ever put on, and so must have seemed terribly insincere by comparison. I was of course familiar with the dirty or dark jokes Denise made after bedtime, and caught the jokes she lobbed over the girls' heads, jokes neither they nor Shasta realized existed. Even disagreeing with Shasta's critique, though, I caught the knowing wink of her question, the one hiding in every TV advertisement: *you* get it. Who doesn't receive a thrill from a secret compliment?

"You know," I said. "Doing lots of fun activities."

My mother visited the girls again with a bowl of Chex Mix. She did not come to Shasta and me, but she did look at me passively, as if she might be trying to identify some realtor she'd seen on a shopping-cart ad. Shasta nodded at her and told me quietly, "Susan's the type of lady who's always thinking about poisoning people's tea, muttering to herself she could do it if she wanted to, nobody would stop her."

"That's awfully judgmental," I said, "but not necessarily inaccurate."

I prepared myself for some unkind question about my daughters, but instead she started talking about herself. She was a beach girl, she said. Kids who stayed up here didn't care about knowing anything. It was too easy to grow pot in the national forest lands, to teach summer people to jet ski and winter people to snowboard. Everyone said the drinking water up here was laced with something, and that was why even people who didn't smoke seemed stoned all the time. To save your brain, she said, you have to escape.

How are your grades? That's how I got out. There's a question I didn't ask. I remember thinking that kids have no idea how simple their trajectories really are, how easy they are to trace. A token resistance to the lifestyle up there was just part of the lifestyle up there. The ones who never talked about getting out were the only ones who got out. And this girl who was worrying about her brain had been a truant since fourth grade. I'm sure she used wadded-up worksheets beneath the kindling of her campfires. A little scholastic prodding from an uncle—how much could it do when her father didn't even read her report cards?

I could have guessed that she'd stay, that she'd drink beer in the woods and fail classes at the community college. Going to bars at nineteen, getting stabbed in the crotch—well, that's more than I anticipated.

"Who did this?" I asked Rick through the phone. "Was it a stranger, some crazy person?"

"Some white fuck who calls himself Indian Steve. The bartender called him her ex-boyfriend. Guy is almost my age." I thought I could hear in his voice that he still had his beard, that his voice had to travel through it. "Crazy? I don't know. Crazy if he doesn't leave town or blow his fucking brains out."

"Big guy?"

"Little guy, jumpy. Got a black mole right in the middle of his forehead I'm going to use as a target."

"Wait, Steve Hillenbrand? He was my year."

"Hope you've got a funeral suit, then."

"No one liked him then, either. He had trouble getting people to take him seriously."

Something like a snort came from the wet beard. "He tried to get everyone calling him Indian Steve," Rick said. "Most just call him Asshole Steve."

"Sounds about right."

"Time I'm done they'll call him Colostomy Steve."

A long moan with a sort of honking quality came through the receiver, like a goose mourning. If she hadn't lost too much blood, her heart would be supercharging to maintain blood pressure; the arteries of her neck would be rearing up like garden hoses, struggling against the choker she was almost certainly not wearing but that I couldn't picture her without. I saw the usual sunny gleam of her tan wiped off the pale base beneath it.

"Hey, Rick? Put your hand on her forehead. What's her skin feel like? Hot? Clammy?"

"Like a fish fillet."

"Obvious question," I said, "but you're driving as fast as you can?"

Every once in a while that old Elton John song "Daniel" comes on the radio. Of all things that could have made me think about Rick, this is what I got. I have my own adapted version, like the silly songs you sing to little kids: *[Rick], my brother, you are older than me / do you [know I] still feel the pain / of the scars that won't heal?* I thought it once, now I'm stuck with it.

You are older than me.

There's a pause after *you are,* then *older than me* is sung as a unit, almost a single word. How charged that phrase is when it comes to brothers, how freighted with implied responsibilities. Before Sacramento, we'd lived in the Berkeley hills. When my brother was nine and I was five, our parents considered themselves at liberty to leave us to our own devices and spent half their weeknights out on the town. My mother would cut up hot dogs in some mac-and-cheese and take off at 4:30 in the Chrysler to meet my dad in Jack London Square. In the mornings we'd all pile in Dad's Mustang, the air in the cab smelling like stale cocktails. He'd drop me and Rick off at school and my mother at her car on his way to work.

My brother, charged with looking after me, had installed a hook-and-eye latch on the inside of his bedroom door and spent most of his time behind it.

One of those nights, fish sticks going cold on the stovetop while I ate a bowl of cereal by myself, the floor started heaving below me. The whole house felt as if it had been buoyed up on a wave, a moment of nauseating weightlessness. The tremor tipped my chair back against the wall and the oak table into my guts, pinning me between the two. My bowl of Cap'n Crunch slid against me without overturning, draping a cold splash of milk and crunch berries on my shirt. The rumbling was still shaking plates on the wall when Rick streaked by toward the back door. It was only as he turned the handle that he glanced over his shoulder. He paused when he saw me pinned there, his panicked eyes met mine, and then he was gone.

A few minutes after the world had calmed down, he came in and shoved the table off of me, and we sat in front of the TV, watching quietly together. Few memories of our aborted brotherhood are so dramatic, of course. And the memories are not so much memories as an agglomeration of neglectful years. Though I'm old enough now to be past measuring people—brothers, mothers—against their ideal versions, I still feel it's fair to judge mine against the average.

My parents had been waiting in line for the Bay Bridge toll-booths when the quake happened. The bridge collapse terrified my mother so viscerally she made us move to Sacramento, which was the beginning of the end for their marriage. I told myself that, as far as I was concerned, I was moving without a brother, and I wanted to believe this lie more than anything. How many more years until I stopped wanting it? Have I stopped wanting it now?

A real brotherhood needs the fire of a shared childhood to form. Is it even possible to build one, now that the forge has cooled?

There are so many versions of this ride tonight. There's the ride Rick's on and the ride I'm on, his side of the phone and mine. There is the truck I see, Rick's old truck, Rick's self as I last saw him, Shasta as I last saw her. There is the truck of reality, which might not even be a truck. There is a ride in which Shasta doesn't make it to the hospital. There is a ride in which she does. There is a ride that ends with him and me saying we'll talk again soon, and meaning it. But these are not the only ways tonight's ride might end. If my estimation is right, he's on one of the stretches of road that runs like a shoestring over the top of a ridge, so steep that even in daylight you have to stick your head out the window and look down to see anything but sky. And if my estimation is wrong, he either hit that stretch five minutes ago, or he'll hit it five minutes from now.

As much as my concocting these different versions may sound like just a bit of mental masturbation, I think of them more like variances in time zones. I'm in Sedate Pacific Time. They're in Retrograde Mountain Time. What would Rick think if I told him about Schrödinger's cat, if I explained the thought experiment? How would he react to the words *thought experiment*?

And since we're playing with time, let's rewind a bit further. Let's see Shasta on a barstool as she turns toward the sound of the opening door and sees Asshole Steve has arrived. This picture is odd, because in my story it's seventeen-year-old Steve Hillenbrand, his oily hair long and slicked back. The black mole above his eyebrow is the size of a gumdrop. Does she smile at him? Or does she grip the bar, make worried eye contact with the bartender? Is Steve able to approach in peace, or does he charge, knife in hand, the moment the door closes behind him? The answers to these questions must matter, my gut tells me, but there's no truth to that. They're all retroactive extrapolations from the same result, which generated the questions in the first place.

Shasta, how right were my predictions for you? And if I saw where you were headed and your father didn't, am I the one to blame for not steering you off that course? The idea of God is nice, but I'd find it easier to believe in an entity omniscient but the opposite of omnipotent. Let's be honest. Adult trajectories are no more difficult to trace. My teachers knew where I was going and were just happier with the answer—or at least the teachers who didn't think I was a prick. And my current trajectory is well and consciously triangulated by the house payments, the college funds, the retirement accounts. The Song of My Mortgage.

That's probably why our dad took so little interest in us after the divorce. We were too easy to predict. There was no thrill of the unknown. And if most lives are like movies whose endings can be anticipated before the close of the first scene, a certain percentage of parents are like the theatergoers ready to walk out on such predictable fare.

Dad liked to take us to movies, actually, and mostly movies we were too young for. That was the one thing he could think of to do: an entertainment for us that would entertain him, too. We sat parallel to each other, staring forward at *Goodfellas*, *Pulp Fiction*, *Silence of the Lambs*, *Unforgiven*. Everyone had a popcorn, and no one could take from anyone else's after he'd finished his own—a rule directed at Rick, who looked like he was holding a softball when he pulled his hand out of a tub. Dad was a partner at a major accounting firm in Sacramento before the divorce. He commuted from Tahoe for a year before starting a ramshackle CPA firm up there catering to small businesses and households. He became obsessed with skiing, and tried to initiate us into the sport, but the trips stopped after two winters of us disappointing him and holding him back. He went on days we weren't there; he never mentioned this, but you could see the wear on his skis. After that, he became as predictable to me as I was to him.

But on this strange night, in my darkened kitchen, here Dad is for his close-up. Jesus, now everything was pouring out of this wound. I won't lie, a part of me wanted to hang up the phone, close it all off like putting a stopper in an oil well. Something of the situation reminded me of when Denise and I were young and newly together, talking late into the night, convinced we could heal our wounds better by picking at them than by leaving them be. How complicated it is, how impossible, to sort out one's feelings toward those early life embarrassments. I long for them at the same time that I long to be further away from them.

Rick said he was coming into South Lake.

"How's Shasta? Can you still feel a pulse?"

"She's still mumbling."

"Making sense?"

"Mother*fuck*er, mother*fuck*er . . . something something . . . mother*fuck*er."

"Makes sense, considering."

"Not too far from my own sentiments."

The kitchen light came on, and I slammed my eyes shut. A little scream muffled itself. Opening them a crack, I saw a blurry shape too small to be Denise. When she spoke I knew it was Chelsea. She was holding the red Spiderman cup she still uses to rinse after she brushes her teeth. She came into focus as I adjusted to the light. She watched my hand as it clapped the phone to my shoulder.

"What is it, kiddo?"

"Daddy?"

"What is it?"

"Is that another woman?"

"Jesus Christ, Chelsea."

"I won't tell Mom."

Her manner bore this out. She seemed entirely unbothered by the prospect. Perhaps interested by it.

"I would hope you would tell your mother. It's your uncle."

Her eyes were unfocused. She was searching her mind for an uncle. His *persona non grata* status was not something she'd been privy to. Like her grandmother, he just didn't come up. I could see her mind turning, thinking I kept a secret line of communication with her uncle in the hours when she was asleep, kept him to myself. She processed a betrayal differently when she thought she was the one being betrayed.

"Get your water and go back to bed."

If she'd wanted water, she would have gotten it in the bathroom. She was out here for a midnight soda or something else off limits. Giving her an out for her indiscretion sped her along. These girls, like me, like the wife I chose, all calculate, plot, and plan, however benignly. When Rick was born he took the good looks and left all the forethought for me.

By the time Chelsea had disappeared back into the dark hallway, I could feel Rick shouting against my pajama shirt. When I put the phone back to my ear, I could hear it was just my name. "Sorry, sorry," I said. I explained about Chelsea.

"We're here. We're going in."

"How is she?"

"The same."

"Rick," I said. "Good luck."

"Hey. *Thank you.* Thanks for staying with me."

When the line went dead, I lost the picture. Once he was off the phone taking Shasta in, it was as though my knowledge of their lives, of everything that had happened in the last forty-five minutes, was contained within parentheses, and I couldn't see anything before or after. Their lives were a fog to me, wholly in shadow. I sat there for a while wondering if I would get a call in the morning, connecting me to an image of Shasta recovering in a hospital bed, her gauze-wrapped legs under a medical gown and a linen blanket, sipping a boxed apple juice. Or perhaps, God forbid, I'd get a darker picture. But no, I thought: if I wanted an update, I would have to be the one to call him. Though I could get the same information from the website of the *Tahoe Daily Tribune*.

It occurred to me that I could drive up to Barton Memorial in two hours, might even be there before she was out of surgery. This was what a brother would do. The idea was intoxicating—driving those dark curving roads in the night, guided by instincts so old they felt like genetic memory. I imagined myself there in the recovery room, explaining to him what happens as anesthesia wears off. I imagined him taking me up in a bear hug, her clasping my hand in thanks. After a while of imagining this, I walked back down the hallway in my pajamas.

In bed, I nestled up to Denise. We hadn't slept this close in years. All the usual complaints: my temperature, her loud breathing, my restlessness, her insomnia. If we aligned ourselves at opposite poles of the mattress, we could each get something akin to a decent night's rest. I remembered how, in the early years, the nightly contact with her had been the deepest salve. The loneliness of solitary sleeping takes years to accrete to the point that another person's sounds and movements are a comfort instead of a curse. But as I curled around Denise that night, she curled into me. I draped my arm across her ribs, and a deep, satisfied breath swelled in her chest.

"Who was that?" she asked.

"No one," I said. "I'll tell you in the morning."

THE UNPLAYABLE ÉTUDES

THE FIRST OF THEM

The first of the études always reminds her of a day when she was thirteen, though there's no reason to remember this one day over so many others like it, while things were still good and summer meant beautiful blue skies with her parents lazing on chaise longues near the docks, her mother sipping Coca-Cola and her father a ginger ale whiskey. Her mother was reading *Under the Sign of Saturn* that month. Occasionally her father would use a copy of a magazine to block the sun from his face, but usually he just turned his head to the side, ambiguously dozing while he baked himself golden. She would have been in the ocher-yellow fiberglass kayak, and her brother, who had the lung capacity, would have been swimming out to the island. This was not the only perfect day, but like any piece of music, she thinks, you can only hear one moment of it at a time.

The first of them does not sound impossible. It sounds, simply, like two distinct pieces of music being played simultaneously, perhaps in adjoining rooms. On the top is a lilting, Mozarty pastoral. She plays it and thinks of the gentle wind rolling on the water and the green coast in the distance, freckled with white cottages. Underneath is a gentle thumping march, someone rapping quietly on an old door. That's the tune of her brother's breaststrokes, powerful enough to cradle-rock the kayak when he passes close by. Here's the difficulty: it's not two pieces for two hands; it's not two separate staves. Some notes for the upper melody come from the left hand, and some from the right. Sometimes it's the right hand knocking, and sometimes it's the left. Playing the pastoral and the march together requires a forced schizophrenia, and at the same time a unity. The impossibility of this first one isn't in the hands. It's in the mind.

How can opposite things exist at once, even in memory? The perfection of that day, then everything after. It took her a long time to be able to play this piece without crying. She plays it and she sees the eleven o'clock sun hanging at a hawk's angle of descent, and her brother's arms crashing through the small swells the breeze made. He was such a strong swimmer.

BAIRD ON LIGETI

She had listened to an interview in which Baird said that the first time he heard Ligeti's *Invention,* it gave him the image of the devil tumbling down an infinite staircase. It was perfectly chaotic, everything out of place just enough to be noticed. It was music that never went where the heart willed it. Calling it Kafka music, as some people did, was reductive. Baird was twenty-three when he heard it. He'd hated avant-garde until then, and he continued to disdain most of the ambitious composers. But he loved the Ligeti. He bought them all, the recordings and the sheet music, and sat at his piano banging away at them, particularly those études known for their difficulty. Étude no. 14a had been deemed impossible for a human player, but Baird threw himself at it nonetheless, over and over. He didn't know if it was too difficult for any human, and he might not be the one to pull the sword from the stone, but he poured his hours into it anyway. It wasn't practice, he said. It was play.

He wanted to take it further. Any fool could write something well beyond the possible. The next art of the piano would be in creating work that teased you into believing it was within your reach, music that seemed to be right there in front of you. Tantalus, he called the collection of études. As he was composing, he thought often of that lonely demigod: the fruit always rising, the water always receding. All these remarks were on the record. Was she naïve to angle her neck upward? Clearly, that was what Baird wanted. He didn't write the damn things for player piano. Still, was the music a grail or a mousetrap? Perhaps Baird was simply graying the space between the two. He never said much about the études—only his one declaration, so simple you'd think English was his second language: "Art should be more difficult." More difficult than what?

CANDELABRUM

Someone has lit a candelabrum on the practice piano backstage. A candelabrum! Is she Liberace? It's Darin who's done it, of course. He's the sweetest man. The sweetest men could also be dolts. Some might suggest a certain doltishness was required. She's never counted the years it took her to realize the Sweetest Man was not what she wanted: it would have been too depressing. One couldn't call oneself a good judge of her own character after that.

How many of the people who dream of having a butler would, if granted one, be constantly mortified in front of him?

Darin had seemed the perfect antidote, though that interpretation came only in retrospect. You cannot see the movement of a symphony from within it. She's never told him about Layla. She knows the worries men get, and how quickly they sink the buoyant fantasies. Men cannot provide everything, nor can they be at peace with *not* providing everything. She won't give him that dark corner of her mind. It is not his to plumb.

All those beautiful brunches: the berries he bought, buckwheat waffles, hand-whipped cream, light-filled Sunday mornings with the most obvious Sunday morning music. It was a heaping half of the life she wanted. He had never made her lie naked, facedown, on the top of her piano. He had never pricked her skin with the long tines of a fondue fork. He did puppy-dumb things like drip wax on ten thousand dollars of piano. She blew out all the candles and touched a knuckle, not a fingertip, to a little gleam at the top of one of them, and she felt it turn into a thicker second skin inside the little folds. The antidote. The antidote to the antidote. What could she do but alternate? She did not want sweetness only. She did not want roughness only. She especially did not want anything in the middle.

HOW HER MOTHER TOOK IT

Like a shattered windshield. Her mother did not fall apart, but she collapsed into a web of opaque pebbles. For the rest of her life she projected an imminent disintegration that never came. She wept for years, of course, at church services and TV commercials and offhand comments and at nothing, but those outbursts were only the surface of her mourning. Exhibit A: days after what would have been his twenty-third birthday, at a dinner in the city with the Patels and the Rosmunds, she improvised a speech about what an asshole Charlie had been sometimes.

"Such an asshole," she said. "I'd tell him to get his dirty shoes off the coffee table, and he'd say, 'Get a life, Mom.' When I told him once how high my expectations were for him, he said it was because I'd given up on myself. You can't say something like that and not be an asshole."

"Marie," her father had said, "he was fourteen."

"Do you mean to suggest, Ben," she replied, "that being a teenager and being an asshole are mutually exclusive?"

Exhibit B: at a church brunch, years after that, she was on her way to cut pound cake, and she froze, standing there with an eight-inch kitchen knife held upright in her hand. At first she seemed to have zoned out, but after two-and-a-half minutes, it looked more like catalepsy. Failed interventions included a soft and then firm calling of her name, a hand on her elbow, snapping in front of her eyes (which did induce blinking), and gentle slaps on the top of her wrist. Only after her father delicately peeled back each finger from the handle and slipped the knife from his wife's hand did she return to life. "Have you ever gotten lost in a train of thought?" she asked.

Exhibit C: a longitudinal study of her conversations. Her mother had always made her and Charlie laugh with adult laughter, and the adults around her laugh with childish laughter. In the early years afterward, her mother's humor was bitter and sometimes elicited smirks but never anything audible. But by the time she was an adult, her mother made no jokes, only smiled with a waspy politeness. As she progressed into her fifties, her mother failed to even recognize jokes.

She remembers dubbing her father, dressed one day in a steel-gray double-breasted suit and a matching vest, the *USS Monitor*, and her mother's dry response: "Why, that's a boat, dear."

She imagines that behind the grim, pale person who keeps the curtains closed and prefers only white flowers, her old mother is tumbling down an infinite staircase, that the notes of life all sound out of place just so. There's the Ligeti again. Another metaphor. It's not a good sign, she knows, when you think about someone you love primarily in metaphors.

THE GENDER OF THE PIANO

In the Spanish it is masculine. In the French it is masculine. In the Italian it is even more masculine: *il pianoforte*. Latin came and went too early. The Germans have come the closest: an upright piano is neuter. A grand, however, is still masculine. Bless the neutered language English: a grand piano can be what it wants—or, some would say, what one wants it to be.

After she announced her program, that old wreck Havelin devoted his column in *Pianist* to a technical analysis of why a woman would never manage Baird's études, let alone be the first. The average man's hand, at 8.9 inches, could not manage the gaps that several of the pieces required, nor could that of a woman in the 99th percentile for hand width (here he made some facile joke about courting a gorilla). He cited a questionable study from the state university of Moldova about the relative speed of synapses in men and women. He cited lore about higher-order thinking.

She let the crowds shout him down for her. She thought about sending him pictures of herself hanging weights from her fingers every day in the kitchen: stretching, stretching. She had taken the pictures. She decided she would send them after the fact.

DIFFERENT IMPOSSIBILITIES

Difficulties of the mind, like those in the first of the *Tantalus* études, some claim, cannot be classified as impossible. The mind is only about as well-mapped as the ocean, they say. Its depths are not known. Besides some apophatic arguments about God, its limits are not circumscribed. She thinks the lack of a map does not erase the territory.

Impossibilities for the hand are the easiest to outline. Some spans are just too wide for a hand that tops out at five fingers. Baird has claimed, somewhat coyly, that his pieces contain no six-fingered chords: "Not if you're clever." But it's not just about sprawling chords. Some call for clusters of four fingers near the top or bottom, with a pinky that has to reach for the ninth above the octave. She's found that in Baird's music there is a quantum uncertainty to the impossibility of reaching any particular note: On a given attempt, your finger might or might not make the stretch. Probability has to be on your side. But in all of the pieces, there are many such stretches. Probability must remain on your side more times than probability can possibly remain on your side.

There is science, too, to back the limitations contained within the piano itself. The quick repetitions of notes in numbers 3, 4, and 7 push the responsiveness of the instrument. Each string vibrates on a wavelength. Strike the hammer too soon and it's like a raw bounce on a trampoline. The string quiets or goes on a chaotic fritz.

And then there is simple endurance. Ravel's *Gaspard de la Nuit* was the famous test of will before Baird decided it was soft. When the quickly repeated notes are grouped into quickly repeated chords, there is no tag-teaming of fingers against a key to sound the note. The whole hand must rise and fall at a rate of blurred vibration that challenges all those minuscule, almost undiscovered muscles in the metacarpal network. No one wants to believe that endurance tests cannot be overcome. It's a culture of sports movies, ultramarathoners, Jamaican bobsledders, and daredevil magicians. She can say this: Any time she's played more than half of them in a stretch she's had to soak her hands in ice baths, and they've still felt the next day as if they had been run over by a delivery truck.

LAYLA

The fondue fork. A kitschy Santa candle she'd inherited from an aunt. A magazine rolled so tightly it looked like a baton. Every time she saw what was coming, she flushed down to her bare hips. Every time it began happening, she felt the glue of gravity seal her seat to the ground or the bed or the piano or the counter. She felt her heart go tachycardic, a seizing hand banging crazed notes against the white keys of her ribs and the sharp black keys between them. She was always mute, stuck between the impulses of surprised laughter and a scream of terror. That was okay. As far as she could tell, Layla wanted her mute. The problem was the hours afterward. Layla left every time: for a walk, for coffee, for another girl in the registry of her phone—she didn't know, and was left with an empty bed in a dark room with a view of the half-lit city, with the pungent pressured air of atomized old sweat. In those hours shame and regret became a literal black fog in her vision, and she'd lie curled up, immobile, blinking into it. She couldn't see the door of her refrigerator or the bright Kandinsky print on the far wall. Her table and its three rough-finished chairs seemed to swim in a swamp. Though sometimes she considered throwing herself out the window, she wouldn't brave stepping off the bed for the fear that, though she knew it was irrational, there were supernatural beasts in the fog. She believes now that she came close to psychosis. Another word for it is delirium. A nicer word. And the truth is she could have lived with the balance, the dark hours weighed against the most vivid in her canon. She was Layla's passenger, and a part of her enjoyed that. Except that Layla was accelerating. The pain she wanted to inflict had to be pushed further. Layla began leaving scars. Not pinpricks but little stripes, and in semi-visible places like the insides of her upper arms. It was the look in Layla's eyes as she did it: no longer cold coals, now more afraid than she was herself—terror, loss of control. Layla never let on much about the life of her mind, but she could see the being inside scrabbling, tumbling, the infinite staircase: there was the Ligeti again.

Detaching required a plan of severance: a secret move to another borough, along with breaking from all mutual friends and places, and almost, she felt, of ideas. Walking alone to a drab new bagel shop, she felt like a part of her brain had been excised. She worried for months about Layla showing up on her street holding a knife, posed just like her mother at that church brunch.

THE COMPUTER SIMULATION

It had not been long before a bored music writer had uploaded Baird's sheet music to be played by a computer and then written three thousand words about it. It was good music, he argued, but when you took away the gimmick, it was second-rate good. It did not make itself immortal. When letters flowed in chastising the man, he made the audio of the computer simulation available on the website.

Another music writer managed to sit with Baird while he listened to it for the first time. "Piss in my coffee while you're at it," Baird was quoted as saying as the opening notes began. He was described by turns as distraught, amused, scornful, and gleefully scornful. He called it a crippled attempt, and he was not referring to the aural limitations of the stereo system. It was the cold logic of the playing. The computer player made the pieces meaningless, Baird said. You could not hear the impossibility.

THE AUDIENCE

Darin is impossible to miss, of course, with a ridiculous bouquet the size of an overstuffed carnival bear. She scans the back for Layla—a ridiculous thought, but that is where she would be standing, improperly attired, if she were to resurface. In every crowd, there's someone who looks like Charlie would have if he'd grown old enough to cultivate a proper beard. It buoys her, sometimes, to close her eyes and imagine that it *is* Charlie, and that she is playing to him. But that is not for tonight. This music is already crowded with ghosts.

She wonders if she could tell, had she more time to scrutinize them, which have come to see her play and which have come to see her fail. Probably not. It's always hard to tell a wolf. Havelin is out there. She can hear his haughty voice surfing the top of the hush. They wear tuxedos and gowns, armor against being interesting.

She pumps the pedals a few times, loosening her feet, and puts one atom of each fingertip against the flat plane of white keys, and listens to the silence become absolute. The last utterances of conversation carom from wall to wall until the curtains soak them up. There is always something dumb about an audience—dumb in the old sense: mute and staring. The opposite of deaf, not just by convention, but by design, by definition. Listening only. Seeing pictures of old gramophones, she always imagines the horn of the player to be a receiver, an ear, when that is the opposite of its purpose. Why is it so comforting, this idea that she could be wrong about everything?

The first étude is already playing. She is glad to be thinking of something else. The undistracted mind creates its own ripples. Still, she tries to listen for a moment, to see if she is keeping Schrödinger's cat both properly alive and properly dead.

HOW HER FATHER TOOK IT

He cried and he didn't at properly surprising times: at breakfast three days later, but not at the wake; at the viewing, but not at the funeral; not at the pool where he went to swim his laps, or anytime he walked down by the docks, but, for reasons no one understood, every time he went to the grocery store. It petered out: a slow curved line that never quite reached its asymptote.

Sometimes it could be years between little meltdowns. Sometimes they seemed to have gone away forever.

Charlie grew mythic, just a touch, in her father's discussions of him. He would have gotten those swim scholarships to Michigan and Stanford. His height chart had never flattened out: Charlie might have spurted past both him and Marie and been the next Michael Phelps. You should have seen him after a meet. He'd put down four cheeseburgers and a bucket of fries. Did you know he wrote poetry? We didn't, but we found it in his journal. Beautiful stuff, truly. It sounded like Yeats.

The next summer he was back in his chaise longue, though now he did read, and what he read was appropriately affirming and humanistic: *Man's Search for Meaning, The Long Goodbye, Tuesdays with Morrie*. "Pablum," Marie said when she was feeling generous. "Dreck," she said when she was not. In this way he became golden again, while his wife turned to salt. He became better in conversation, more philosophical and circumspect. His laugh was less frequent, but it now had an anchor. Though she tries not to, she sometimes resents him for being improved by tragedy.

Some have said he grieved perfectly.

PERFORMANCE

She sweats. It is not a sexy, shimmery sweat. It is not a surprise. She made the strategic choice not to wear white. Regardless, she feels it highlighting the hotspots of her body in scalloped penumbras of wet cloth. She remembers Billie Jean King running Bobby Riggs around the court on the marionette strings of her angle-work. She imagines the cockpit chair of Sally Ride vibrating into space strapped to a million pounds of rocket thrust.

The room is quiet. She knows only that she is playing, that she is creeping along the staff four beats at a time. In the moment there is no telling if she's also rising up into the ether. But she divides her mind properly for the first étude, and that allows her a foothold, a first step up onto the impossible road. Midway through, her fingers feel like boiled hot dogs. The heat radiating from them warms her face. In the last études, which become more mazelike and branch in many paths, her vision blurs and her brain aches. The air is always thin, she thinks, in the rarefied frontiers of the atmosphere. At this point only memory and dull habit guide her through the woods.

She's gasping for breath when she finishes. Sweat drips from her elbows to the piano bench in quick little *plop plop plops* that land in 3/2 time. She should stand and offer some pageantry: a bow, a sweep of the arm. Forget that, she thinks. She's not going to stand up until she has to. She stares instead at the ring finger of her left hand. At the top left corner, where the nail meets the skin, is a tiny drop of frank red blood. Each of her fingertips is underlaid with a light purple bruise. Only she knows whether or not she has brought it off, but if the audience stands, if they applaud, how much does it matter?

TONAL VS. ATONAL

The argument has been put forward that atonal music has a lower bar of difficulty than tonal music because in tonal music an audience can tell when a note is out of place. The argument is that atonality is a veil. If the devil is tumbling down a staircase, will an audience take note of how many steps he misses? She thinks this is an evasion. She knows Ligeti well enough that she can hear when someone fumbles.

The two styles present divergent philosophies. Music should comfort. Music should discomfit. People should be comforted. People should be jarred from comfort. Binaries again. *Gaspard de la Nuit* is rapid and bustling but still founded upon a resonation with the expectations of the mind. *Invention* is like going mad. Like being driven mad.

Atonality may offer the veil, but tonality provides a blanket. Atonal: like being pinned mute and naked to the piano in front of all those people. Tonal: buoyed by the music, which has its own soul.

Tantalus is mostly tonal. Some études are rousing, some sweeping, some surprisingly gentle given the difficulty. Even an untrained listener will have the sense of where a piece is going. But tucked in the score are chords and notes and phrases that are paths to nowhere. Anyone who knows his or her theory will pick up the cues, and even as the tenth étude ends will be left waiting for those phrases to resolve. Anyone who can't help but wait for resolution risks waiting forever.

QUESTIONS

How can opposite things exist at once, even in memory? Grief and persistence. Retreat and embrace. Music and silence. With the averages tipped so far toward silence it's a wonder a single sound can catch. Art should be more difficult. More difficult than what? Is she Liberace? She sweats enough without fur coats, but is it there, in the announcements, the challenges, the gauntlets thrown? Grief and persistence. Retreat and embrace. What could she do but alternate? There is no going forward past a certain bond of caretaking and niceties, no going back to the terrible days she misses more than anything. Sometimes she feels there is nothing more ahead. Is that why it is so comforting, this idea that she could be wrong about everything? She reminds herself there is no forward or back, only ever the one moment: now, the standing, sweat-soaked; the bow. She has pulled it off. She hasn't. Only she knows whether or not she has brought it off, but if the audience stands, if they applaud, how much does it matter? Some will say she played perfectly.

Oh, Charlie—what would you say? A question too foolish to even ask, but that's exactly what she's done.

AS LONG AS THE LAUGHTER

Dov is already sweating when he takes the stage. It's not nerves, not after all these years. Adrenaline, he calls it. Or just fat, sweaty middle age. "Omaha," he says. He shakes his head dismissively. Their response is warm enough. "Usually I say something good about the city I'm in. You'll give me a pass on that, right?" Laughter throughout. This opener plays well everywhere but the major metros and the South. His first hard lesson learned when he started touring years ago: make fun of the South, but never in the South. Midwesterners, at least the kind that come to comedy shows, won't trust you unless you insult them. "I mean, you guys understand. You live here. You didn't pay me to blow sunshine up your ass." Then into the bit suggesting if anyone ever did offer, in the literal sense, to blow sunshine up his ass, he'd do it in a heartbeat. "Really? You're going to pass on that? It sounds fantastic." They like the ass humor. Good thing. Plenty more of it to come.

"Kind of a college town, Omaha. Young crowd? Young people, make some noise."

He holds out his microphone and the auditorium fills up with howling. He brings it back to his face to quiet them.

"Old people, go 'Ah, fuck it.'"

Laughter. He leaves a little pause. Lets them wonder what's next.

"You guys think sex is fun?"

The roar this time is even louder. His ears go tinny. He quiets them again.

"Yep," he says. "Definitely a young crowd."

"Enjoy it while it lasts, kids. You've got maybe five years."

"People my age, we don't have sex for fun. We just have sex because, I don't know, it's just something we're supposed to do, like going into work, except with a much greater chance of humiliation." He describes how he looks naked: like an unbaked loaf of sourdough. Smells like it too, he says. The latter is untrue, but the former accurate: he stood naked in front of his full-length mirror for forty-five minutes one day, brainstorming similes on a yellow legal pad. Not the most fun day, scrutinizing his terrible body, hunting for language vivid enough to convey just how ugly it was. The runner-up is that his belly looks like a bunch of pugs taped together. Too surreal, he thinks, so he's only testing it in smaller venues.

He's known for this: the self-scrutiny, the guilt, the shame. His persona—a failure, an out-of-shape, hypocritical, amoral, sexually deviant divorcée—is seeded in truth, and the rest of the jokes flow forth from it, carrying the weight that makes it convincing. Because he's laughing along, because he makes it effortless, because it's not about them. People think it's easy standing up there deconstructing himself for an hour. They're right only to the extent that comedy is like a sport, no time to dwell on anything while the clock runs, just enough mindspace free to do quick assessments and make minor adjustments. When you walk off the stage it feels like you just went on a minute earlier. What gets him is the rest of the night, the bar or the hotel, where he replays the jokes in his mind and is now just the butt of them, rather than the teller. His second hard lesson: the thrill of the laughter lasts only as long as the laughter.

"My back looks like a big cheese pizza. You know the cheap kind, with all the brown bubbles? A woman I hooked up with a few months back asked if I wanted to videotape it so we could watch it later. *What*? It's going to look like two pig carcasses slapping together. Of course I don't watch to watch it."

"Why would we make a record of this?"

They've got the lights a little too bright on him. The sweat is coming through, though that's normal enough. Every set has some jokes about the sweating, a preemptive strike. The auditorium out in front of him is black, except for the twilit faces in the first two rows.

He can't see her, the girl who will approach him that night at the bar. She'll wait by the venue's side door and follow his cab to TGI Friday's. Before she heads in, she'll sit in her car for fifteen minutes to give him some time to settle in, to text her friends about what she's going to do, and to work up the courage she pretends to never need. He'll notice her fashionable outfit first, just black tights and a belt around a low-cut purple blouse. And the boots, of course. She knows no man can resist expensive boots. When he sees her he'll set eyes on her face, the youthful glow and the evocative makeup, the pageant smile, and then, not knowing she will be coming toward him, that he will soon be interacting with her, his gaze will drift downward to admire the way those tights reveal the body underneath. When she perches on the next stool over and turns that smile like a spotlight on him, he'll think: trap set, trap sprung.

"Buy me a drink?" she'll say.

"I'm the famous one," he'll reply. "You buy me a drink."

So she'll wave the bartender over and ask for a whiskey sour for herself and a cosmopolitan for her friend. When he asks for ID she'll shrug in feigned embarrassment: "I forgot it." *Well, go get it* is the only response she'll get.

"Oh, hell no," Dov will say, trap unsprung. But then she'll smile at the bartender, take some long blinks, and ply him with a voice growing more girlish by the moment, and soon the trap is resprung, though he's considering the metaphor of chewing his own leg off and how it would apply in this situation. Punching himself in the nuts?

"You should just leave. I don't like you," he'll say, and she'll laugh.

"I'm not over twenty-one," she'll say, leaning toward him, "but I am over eighteen."

Since the show went on air, there have been run-ins like this, though never one so blatant. When she puts her driver's license down on the bar in front of him—her birth date is in 1993, making her twenty—he's going to want to tell her this isn't fair, what she's doing. She's in that tiny sliver of life where her body is like a miracle, the limbs so slender, the breasts so perky, the waist so small and perfectly shaped that her figure's like an ultramodern work of architecture that, sculpted from some futuristic polymer, doesn't look like it should be able to hold itself up. He'll want to say that because she hasn't reached the age where fat starts depositing itself like bad debt all over the body, she has power. That she's abusing it by sitting here next to him.

He'll know how to take himself out of the equation: all he has to do is say no and maintain it. But he'll also be aware of the sharkish thoughts his balls are sending to his brain: never before in his life has he had someone so young and beautiful; if she's offering, is it wrong to take? Thousands of years of human evolution have been training him to say yes to this exact proposition.

And there it will be on a platter, as she interrupts his thoughts by leaning forward to whisper in his ear: "I want you to fuck me." She will get an unexpected thrill from saying this so directly. With boys from her college she lets her interest remain unsaid, lets the context ferret it out, and she'll start to wonder if that isn't because their desire is so overt, compared to Dov's, whose hesitation she can sense. It's something she will want to use in the future, this statement, as direct as knocking on a door. That is the feeling she is hunting tonight, the feeling that there are things to learn about herself that the boys at U Nebraska just can't teach her.

She'll look at him. He'll look at her, and then at his hands on the bar.

But all that's later. During his set the girl sits somewhere in the dark of the middle-back-left with strangers on either side of her, one hand resting a little too high to be proper on the inside of her upper thigh. She knew what she wanted to do as soon as tickets went on sale. She's watched the first season and has what she thinks is a sense of his life. His attempts at dating: bizarre, quixotic, embarrassing. One-night stands with women who snore during sex or turn out to be truck drivers. To her, these are dispatches from the field, warnings from the future. It's sexy to her when he derides his body, when he talks about how abject middle-aged sex is. Not one man has ever said these things to her. More so, there are hints of the truths he's telling already creeping into her experience. When the boys she's had, both the boyfriends and the one-offs, roll off her after five minutes of robotic hammering, she never feels exultant like women on TV, never rolls her eyes back into her head and smiles at the ceiling. She just looks up, hands crossed over her sternum, wondering what more it takes to be happy.

He's got her answer.

"The closest most of us get to happiness is getting used to unhappiness."

"I'm unhappy all the time, but it doesn't really bother me anymore. I'm so used to unhappiness I kind of think happiness would ruin my life. I'd be like, do you have any idea how long it took me to build that mountain of misery and self-loathing? Now I have to start over."

"Couldn't be a comedian anymore. Know what kind of gigs a happy comic gets? Birthday clown."

"Since I turned forty my knee just hurts. Hurts to walk on it, hurts to stand on it. It's not a medical condition—my doctor just said, 'it happens'—and I'm used to it now. If the pain went away, here's how it would change my life: now when I was sitting on my couch at home, I'd feel bad that I wasn't doing any exercise. I wouldn't go out jogging because my knee works again, but I'd know that I could. My guilt would increase. That's the end result if my health improves. More guilt."

True about his knee, mostly. His doctor didn't seem to care much, but he did identify the problem: Dov's used up all the cartilage on his right side. Dov doesn't really know how that happened:

he's never been a hiker, never played sports. He's done plenty of walking around the city, climbed the stairs to lots of walkups. That must be enough, he supposes. He has an alternate set of jokes about the knee: How did he wear out the cartilage on one side but not the other? Has he been taking more steps with the right leg? Did he play too much hopscotch as a kid? The physical part of that joke is what sells it, hopping on one leg across the stage, but the pain is too severe to do it on the right leg anymore, and he's started to worry about expending the last of his cartilage on the left. When that goes, he'll walk like an old man. Then he'll be the old dog, dragging its back legs, that needs to be put down.

His assessment of his happiness is also not far off the mark. He wouldn't mind being happier, but he really is used to life as is. Truth is, he only feels at ease these days around other comedians, sitting around a table at a pub, joking not about himself but about life in general. Busting someone else's balls for a change. At this point in the tour, he and his two openers are tired of each other's company. The road is draining. Ben heads to his room early after shows to Skype with his family. Dennis goes to trendy bars to get free drinks and pick up young women. Women have always been difficult to be around for Dov: too much grappling for control, too much deciphering of coded messages. And now with the show, the tour, and an HBO special coming up, the pressure for new material is so pressing that any time he gets to himself he spends tirelessly dissecting his own mistakes and failures, sifting out the ones that can be made funny from the ones that can't.

He goes to the chain-restaurant bars to talk with the bartenders and maybe some crusty regulars. Every bartender is an undercover comedian. In that way, it will disappoint him the night the beautiful young girl—she says her name is Jenna—approaches him. Jenna won't be able to tell him anything about the Mets. Jenna will have nothing interesting to say about the state of Nebraska. He could try to talk to her like a normal person, like the guy serving his cocktails, but shows are exhausting—an hour straight just talking under the lights, plus a fifteen-minute encore—and it's so much work with young people discerning what parts of them are bland, what parts are posturing, what parts are genuine philosophies derived from their life experiences and what parts are just platitudes recycled from rock stars he's too old to know anymore.

So when he does the easy thing and switches back into comedian mode, he'll know he's going to take her to bed. That too is the easy thing, the decision not hard to explain to his friends or the guy behind the bar or even himself. *My id had my superego in a headlock,* he'll tell people. *She was young, hot.* This will be just a moment after she's told him directly: "I want you to fuck me." That one bald sentence will be powerful enough to conjure an image of them in the act, an image with her in the center and him closer to the edge of the frame, out of the central focus, a blur of lumpy, pale negative space.

When he turns into a performer his posture will straighten. His shoulders will uncoil, and he'll seem a little taller.

"How do you know I don't have AIDS?" he'll ask.

"You don't have AIDS."

"How would you know?"

"It would have been in your set."

You're absolutely right, he'll think—such a horrible thing he could only deal with it by joking, and a wealth of jokes would stem from it. Even simple understatement would do it: *AIDS,* hand on his hip, wagging his head at the crowd, *just my luck.* So she has some insight, he'll think, and he'll want to tell her simply that it makes him sad how right she is, and at the same time to guard that truth from her. *Hands off my suffering. Get your own*: a first draft of a response he'll immediately discard as too revealing.

His hesitation will flush her with pride. Keeping him against the ropes will suddenly be more important than fucking him or learning a life lesson or acquiring a story to record in the online journal she updates in sporadic bursts. She'll ask him to tell her a secret. He'll fire back with "So what's your angle, anyway? Child support?

Paparazzi? Some kind of starfucker blog?" He'll smile when he says it, but she'll sense the hostility behind the question.

"Naïveté," she'll say. "Plain and simple."

"Naïveté indeed. Were I to do the thing you said you want me to do, which is wrong on so many levels, you would see things you can't unsee and feel things you can't unfeel."

"Like being humped by a loaf of sourdough?"

"*Uncooked* sourdough. Can you imagine that and want anything to do with it?"

She will imagine it—something in all her planning she's never done—him on top of her, grunting and sweating, his baggy midsection audibly slapping against hers, and find she's not repulsed. Perhaps she should be repulsed, she'll think, but she finds it endearing. In the scene she pictures, he'll be shy and apologetic during sex, and she'll comfort him and move against him and take the reins and touch his cheek. In that moment she'll think she could be attracted to any body type, that under the right conditions or in the right mood she could be turned on by someone fat or scrawny, hopelessly short or dented with a weird concave chest. She'll feel she understands suddenly how women with fat husbands can stand to go to bed with them, something that's always mystified her before.

"Yes," she'll say, simply, honestly.

"Naïveté indeed," he'll say, touched by the sentiment, wanting more than anything to run away.

He talks about fear during his set as well. "I'm scared of everything," he says. "Spiders. Clowns. Dentists. Everyone's scared of those things. Clown dentists—don't ask. My dad had a dark sense of humor. Spider-clown dentists. I just thought of that, but it's pretty fucking scary, right?"

"Imagine a spider with a clown face, crawling toward you with a drill and that hook thing."

"Tell that to your kids and they'll shit their pants."

"Other people's babies are the scariest thing. Friends always want me to hold their babies, and I don't want to do it. I just don't want to. They're too fragile. It's because I have this weird fantasy—maybe fantasy is the wrong word—this idea that I'll be holding the baby and it will just crack in half like an egg. And then they'll look at me like, 'Holy *shit*, what did you do?' and I'll be like 'I don't know, it just cracked in half.' And they'll be like 'Babies don't just crack in half.' And I'll just shrug like, 'What can I say?'"

"I'm scared of my life changing, because it feels like every decision I've made in my professional and personal life has been a huge mistake." This part relies on a big shit-eating grin. The audience has to buy that this really is a source of amusement for him. Some jokes run on empathy. He suspects that many people, perhaps even most people, feel this way: that their life is a series of errors in judgment. He sees some of the heads in the front row nodding. The bad comedians, the jock comics, the shock comics, the goofsters, never do this—bond with their audience over a shared negative experience—but it's this moment, he feels, that they'll remember. It's in the hush that settles in after the laughter. "If there's a change coming down the pike," he says, "it's not going to be positive." It's the closest thing to a gift he can give them, the promise that all this can be laughed about.

He'll be too scared to undress Jenna in the hotel that night, scared that he'll get the sudden urge to be physically rough with her, or that she'll instinctively recoil when he touches his palm to her ribcage. So he'll sit on the edge of the bed, untying his shoes like a husband getting home from work. She'll stand there, tall in her leather boots, waiting for his next step. When he goes to his belt, still not looking at her, she'll pull the blouse over her head, and he'll take a small comfort in the way her tights reach so high up on her waist they cover her belly button and something about it looks silly. She'll take off her boots to take off her tights, and standing in front of him in just her panties, she'll ask him if he wants the boots back on. He'll shake his head, still looking at the floor.

His reluctance to take off his white underwear will be sad to her in a way that's not endearing, but she'll slide them off him anyway.

He'll tell her, "I don't want to be on top." He won't go into detail, but he hates the idea of his gut hanging onto her flat belly. It's fair enough with women over thirty-five, women ranging from poochy to just plain round, but it will seem like too awful a memory to brand onto a twenty-year-old girl who still believes in good in the world.

Riding him will be an underwhelming experience for her. She will think that word exactly: *underwhelming*. He's not repulsive, as he makes himself out to be, no look or smell of bread dough, just a normal guy in his forties with some extra weight on him. But she will want some intensity of emotion or a moment of humor—she loves to laugh during sex, but no boys can make it happen, and in fact none of them try. Instead she'll find him constantly retreating. She'll look for the mischievous glint that, during their exchanges at the bar, lit up his eyes, but he'll have them squeezed shut as if anticipating a vaccine shot.

After they finish, she'll pull the condom off him, tie a knot in it, and throw it on the carpet near the waste bin. They'll lie in tandem, facing the ceiling, their limbs not touching, two snow-angels too bored to keep going. Her mind will harken back to his routine from the show about sex between people over thirty, how deeply unsatisfying it is. She'll think, *He made it seem like it was funny*. He'll observe her disappointment and regret already that, if this was always going to turn out poorly, he might at least have relished the experience. He'll wish for another go, a chance to redeem himself. He'll imagine her staying the night and him waking her up with kisses and caresses in the morning for round two. That's not where this is going, he'll know.

"Now you know," he'll say.

"Naïveté indeed," she'll say.

"Maybe this is the first in your series of errors in judgment."

She'll look into his eyes and smile gently. "How did you learn to laugh about it?"

"I didn't," he'll say. "I learned to fake it."

She'll turn her face back up toward the ceiling, thinking hard about something, a connection her mind is trying to make. She'll tell him, "When I played youth basketball, my coach always said, 'When you compete, you either win or you learn.'" She'll be flattered when this gets a belly laugh out of him, though she didn't mean it as a joke.

"That's a good philosophy," he'll say. "But it's a terrible thing to tell someone after sex."

She'll laugh too. It will be the kind of laugh that makes her close her eyes, that rocks her in the ribs and curls her toes. This will be the first laugh they've shared that one hasn't extorted from the other. He'll laugh at her laughter, at the absurdity of her naked body lying there, rippling with it. A naked body, even one like hers, doesn't look good laughing. It doesn't have to.

When he thanks the crowd and tells them how great they were and says good night, it's a formality. There's always an encore these days, and though sometimes he just wants to go back to his room or drop a few bucks on a cocktail, he's not immune to the compliment. He sits backstage in a chair with armrests, letting his head roll back and bringing a bottle of water intermittently to his lips. He can hear it clearly: first amorphous cheering, then the chant—"Dov! Dov! Dov! Dov!"—then an accompaniment of stomps and claps in rhythm. He rides it like a high for ten minutes. The promoter comes by and tells him it was great, fantastic.

He has a new energy when he returns to the stage. He always does, and he's built the bit off that. He walks out with a big grin and some spring in the step.

"You guys are the only people in my life who want me back when I go."

"When I was still married, I listened at the front door one time when I left. My wife said, 'Love you,' when I was headed out. Then after the door closed, she said, 'I hope you get hit by a bus, you son of a bitch.'"

"Well, I showed her."

"We had some good years, though. Ever try to hold onto something good? It's like trying to hold onto a cat. A cat who hates you. Who has a moral objection. Now, cats are not easy to catch. But if you try and hold onto one, you are courting death. They'll claw here: the carotid—here: the femoral. You'll look like the end of a Scorsese film."

"Bad things, though, they cling to you. Anybody have a bad job?"

He holds out the mike: some cheers, a lot of shouted *yeahs*, one louder and higher pitched than the others, screaming: "Tell it, brother."

"I will. I will tell it," he says. "You been in that job a long time?"

Laughter.

"I know it," he says. "My job is terrible."

"Bad jobs, they're like those face-huggers from *Alien*. They jump on your face and hold on and shove something in your throat that you really don't want in there. Bad jobs, bad girlfriends, bad boyfriends. That's why, if you look back on your life, the only relationships you remember fondly are the short ones. You meet this amazing person, right? Then after a few weeks they get a sense of your personality and they're like, 'Fuck it, man. I'm outta here.'"

"Bad things hold onto you longer. A bad marriage can transcend time and space."

"But good things last longer. Not while they're going on, but the way they live in the rest of your life. You have a bad job, the day you quit, as soon as you walk out of that store or office or whatever, you get relief. When I go to my spider-clown dentist, I feel relieved as soon as I get up out of the chair. You stand up, and the fear evaporates."

"Good things, you can hold onto those forever. Some of you out there, I know, remember the first person you were in love with. It's probably not the person you're here with tonight."

"You have to look at your date now and deny it," he says, grinning. "Go ahead. I'll give you a minute."

"That's a different kind of love, and you're happy to have it. But sometimes, when he's asleep and you aren't, you think back on it, you remember that guy smiling at you. You remember holding hands running through a cornfield or some other Nicholas Sparks bullshit. And maybe there's a sense of loss with it, but you've got it. Isn't that amazing? You've still got it swimming around up there, along with that squeaker of a basketball game you won, or the first time you got high, or that time you went skinny dipping. Or that time you had sex with a sheep."

"No? Just me?"

"It's like a diamond you get to carry around. A mental photo album that doesn't just have pictures but little slices of the feelings you felt in those moments. That's what comedy is to me. Not necessarily the TV show and the big crowds, but the moments that planted the seed. The way my friends laughed at jokes I made in high school. No one else in my family could make my dad laugh. Just me. And it was this big, meaty laugh like you'd hear out of a drunk Viking. And I could summon it at will."

"He's dead now, you know."

"Shit happens."

"But because I've got the memory—I mean, forty years later and I can remember just how it sounded—he isn't."

This wrap-up isn't funny, but it isn't for them. He's been giving to them for an hour and a half now. He needs one point where he takes something back, something for himself. Free counseling, he'll say if anybody asks. One true good thing.

An interviewer once asked Dov if he'd ever considered suicide, given how focused his act was on his own his own unhappiness. "Murder, yes. Suicide, no," he'd answered. Another deflection. The words weren't false, but the flippant way they came out was. That was the performer, casting no shadow. The times he was starting out and couldn't get a paying gig; his dad's long convalescence in a home; the months leading up to his divorce, with those hours of awful, dismissive paperwork: he'd been angry and overwhelmed and so, so unhappy, but he'd never wanted to do himself in. Not only had he not planned anything but he hadn't thought or fantasized about it the way some people do. He's estimated that he was more unhappy during those times than many people who actually made attempts.

He's thought about it since—you couldn't say frequently, but often enough—not suicide, but why it's so easy for him to say no to it, why for him it fails to exist in the realm of possibilities. It's what he thinks about as he grabs his coat from the rack backstage, and what he's often thought about after his encores this tour. The closing note forms a natural trench that his thoughts can't avoid following.

It's cold enough that he turns up his collar before the door has slammed behind him. The cab he's requested idles near the curb, chuffing exhaust in idyllic puffs that make him think of Christmas. A girl with a cigarette seems to be watching him from under the streetlight on the corner, her eyes following him without interest. A hot young thing from a different world than his. *There's the future and there's the past,* he thinks. He wants to arrive at some insight about the two, but after a minute the best he can come up with is *Fuck 'em both.* He gets in the cab, and they creep out onto the avenue, and maybe he's being an old man about it, but the cars out on the road seem reckless tonight, some of their drivers drunk, some only tired, all of them collisions just waiting to happen. He gives the driver cross streets, and the man nods without saying anything. Dov hears a chattering, and for a moment thinks the man has a little radio in his ear before he recognizes it as a Bluetooth headset. Whoever is on the other end must be saying something funny, because the cab driver gives off a long, slow chuckle, so low and so dark it's like he's laughing in a different language.

EVERY FACE IN THE CROWD

Deckinger had a painting by Evan Durant in his foyer, one of the larger canvases, maybe four feet by six feet. How much it had cost him I didn't know, but I knew other Durants, smaller Durants, had sold for more than thirty thousand. None of my friends could boast a foyer, let alone thirty large to decorate it. Rounding the corner into his living room I was confronted with a kind of optical mystery: the condo, which from its little brick façade should have been cozy if not cramped, was as spacious as the house I grew up in. That's the type of magic money can make. A part of me hated coming to Beacon Hill, because I started to see price tags on everything: on the Durant, on Deckinger's artisan dinner table and matching leather couches and the beveled lowball glass out of which he drank an amber liquid I didn't want to know the price of. He had poured a glass for me as well. It tasted like a winter cake with candied fruit.

"I don't know my spirits very well."

"Cognac," he said. "Paul Giraud."

He surprised me by having the tact not to talk up the drink or say how much he'd paid for the Durant. I'd brought a portfolio for him to look at, and I set it on the table. He flipped through it quickly, then said he'd thought I would bring some of the actual pieces.

"Pumpkins?" I said. "You wanted me to haul pumpkins here on the T?"

"How do you deliver the finished product?"

"That's just one at a time."

"Well, that's thinking a bit small, isn't it?"

He wanted to play with me, to pique my artistic humors.

"You looked me up, Mr. Deckinger. Saw one of my carvings in your neighborhood, right? Consider that a sample."

"Victor Newburn, and I really had to wring it out of him."

Newburn was Chair of Humanities at Harvard, and lived the next street over. He had commissioned me for a jack-o'-lantern mock-up of the famous statue of the Laocoön priest and his sons being strangled by Poseidon's serpents, one of the more interesting assignments I'd taken. I'd ended up needing two pumpkins to encompass the horizontal spread of the tableau.

"I'm offering you a fairly big job. Ten pumpkins, five across, two high. A real panorama of Boston: the skyline, Back Bay, the Hancock, the Pru, the Charles with maybe a sailboat or two. But a knockout job."

"You realize Halloween is this Saturday?"

"Let's be honest. I really want to kick Newburn's ass."

"You want to kick his ass . . . with art?"

"Art's got to have some utility, right?"

"You know I charge five hundred for a pumpkin? Ten pumpkins is five thousand dollars."

"Do I get some kind of bulk discount?"

I looked around at the rich accoutrements of his condominium and took another sip of his cognac. "No. Do you know anyone else who does this?"

He smiled. It was the answer he'd been looking for. I told him I'd draw up a contract, but that I'd need enough up front to cover the cost of the pumpkins themselves. He fished his wallet from his back pocket and handed me twenty-five hundred in cash. "Half now, half on delivery." He noted that I'd seemed interested in the painting in his foyer and encouraged me to admire it for as long as I liked on my way out.

Like every Durant since 1996, it was a painting of a crowd, this one a Tokyo crosswalk at the end of the workday, thousands of identical black suits approaching each other and passing like the densest school of fish. It was painted from the perspective a few feet above, as if someone had stood on a ladder to view the scene, and the style was almost photorealistic—in fact, it appeared photorealistic from more than five feet away, and all the Durants we'd seen in class had seemed that way on the projection screen.

A fellow student had derided Durant as *Where's Waldo?* for grown-ups, and the rest of the class, myself included, had lazily agreed. Professor Wei said we'd have to stand in front of one to understand, and he was right. From afar it looked simply like a picture of a crowd taken without any regard to composition, the entire canvas filled with people. "There's no central focus, no *subject*," I'd said in class. But in the foyer, as I stepped closer, I saw that each face was a focal point, that everyone in that crowd, maybe two hundred people within the frame, had a unique expression. I first looked at a young man glowing with ambition. He'd done something praiseworthy in his office that day. Another owed money to a friend, and another was drunk already, leaving work. I went from face to face, gleaning their stories. Preoccupation, delight, every state of humanity perfectly rendered. Each visage could have been a painting in its own right. As Professor Wei had said, "Every face is *in* the crowd, but no face *is* the crowd." No wonder a new canvas only hit the market every few years.

I walked through Beacon Hill back toward the T station, sure I was going to be robbed. I squeezed the lump of cash to make certain it didn't slip out of my pocket somehow, fearful that if I took my hand out the wad of bills would come out with it and fall directly into a storm drain. Such are the puckish proportions a critical mass of hard money can take on to one underfamiliar with it.

Beacon Hill was beautiful, and it made me angry. It was postcard Boston, with rows of red-brick condominiums with quaint porches, strung in places with ivy, narrow cobbled streets, and little walkable alleys. I'd seen a news item the year before about a parking spot in Beacon Hill selling for a hundred and fifty thousand dollars. John Kerry had a house there, and Uma Thurman. Daniel Webster and Oliver Wendell Holmes Jr. had lived there. The people making art in this city did not: they lived in Jamaica Plain, Chinatown, Dorchester, Roxbury, and Somerville. Their apartments weren't made of brick, and there was no hint of ivy. It wasn't fair that everyone in the most beautiful part of the city was a moneymaker, that one had to buy his way in. The rest of my walk to the station, I thought of how different a world it would be if that Durant lived instead with whoever loved it the most.

I began as an undergraduate at Boston University in 1996, and moved into a three-bedroom apartment in Allston with four other guys. Coming from a suburb of a suburb of Champaign, Illinois, I thought Allston was the heart of the city. With Korean restaurants and record shops and Blanchards liquor (even though I was too young to shop there), how could it not be? And since my friends had gone to UIUC, if not community college, if not no college at all, I saw myself as a grand adventurer, as a very rare individual. My four roommates and I were the type to migrate from the country to the city.

On move-in day Commonwealth was clogged with station wagons and U-Hauls, the sidewalks impassable, and bodies in the B Line trolleys were crammed against the windows. It was a bit harder to see myself as very rare after that, but a kid can do much to restore his illusions if he sets himself to the task. The city was like a contest to see who could make it and who couldn't, and my major in art was a constant competition, one in which I acquitted myself well.

For graduate school I moved to Chinatown. Professor Wei's family had just moved an aunt out of a tiny studio, and they were renting it for five hundred. A twin bed wouldn't fit, so I made use of the cot the professor's aunt had left. That October, in an attempt to fool myself that the cramped space could be made homey, I carved a pumpkin like we'd always done in my home growing up. As an art student now, though, I thought I'd better do something more than a squiggly smile and two round eyes, so I set out to see if I could make a pumpkin look like the Mona Lisa. I threw out the first two drafts, though the second was passable. On the third I found I was able to carve a pumpkin that didn't just look like Mona Lisa but projected the same feeling as the painting, the haunting smile and the wandering gaze. It went up in my window, the only jack-o'-lantern in Chinatown.

A few days later, a man in a neatly tailored suit knocked at my door. I thought I was in trouble for something. He introduced himself as Juan Pacheco, a venture capitalist who happened to like the pho joint downstairs from my apartment and had seen my handiwork. When he asked how much I'd charge to do a pumpkin of Bob Marley, I told him I was too busy with a class project to take on anything else. He leaned in to take a quick survey of the size and condition of my apartment.

"Look," he said, "what's a month's rent for you?"

That was two days before last year's Halloween. I didn't pick up any more clients then. Really, I didn't think of Pacheco as a client but rather as an eccentric windfall. But the following October I started getting calls not just from Pacheco but from his friends and from other acquaintances who'd been to his Halloween party last year. "Can you do Charlie Chaplin?" they asked. I did Picasso's *Guernica* and a Dali clock. I did the Yosemite Valley for a homesick Californian.

A kid carving a pumpkin sees two media: the pumpkin and the empty spaces. As I settled in I learned how many more there were: the orange of the outer shell; the creamy yellow of the rind, which on its own could be carved into intricate designs; the empty spaces; the shadows created by carefully placed recesses; areas of the inner cavity lit by the candle flame; areas through which the flame could be seen directly; effects that could be created by the placement of multiple candles. By the end I could create warmth or silence, movement or stillness, and I could make the eyes of a portrait twinkle. Most pumpkins I could finish in a half a day. The Laocoön took two.

I had three days to carve Deckinger's ten-gourd skyline, two of which I was scheduled to work at the art supply store. My manager was furious that I called in sick for two shifts directly preceding a holiday, but as my pumpkin income meant I no longer had to steal my painting supplies from the store, I felt karmically balanced about it. I'd had thirty-three sales that October. To manage all those jobs, I'd been carving three or more pumpkins a day for the last ten days. I'd developed a preservation regimen as well. With a bleach bath, a coat of petroleum jelly, and a sprinkling of silica beads, I could get a carved pumpkin to last two weeks. That work had netted me seventeen thousand dollars, which was almost as much as I made per year at the shop. The Deckinger commission would put me up to twenty-two.

I walked down Newbury Street to find a model for the panorama from one of the watercolor artists who hawked their paintings of Fenway and the swan boats and Faneuil Hall to tourists. I picked out an eight-by-ten of the Charles with the Mass Ave Bridge and Back Bay behind it. Like all watercolors, let alone all street art, it was lacking in detail, but it gave me the bones, and the rest would be easy enough to embellish.

"How much for this?" I asked. None of the pictures had a price tag.

"Forty," said the man wearing a black pageboy hat and cheap button-down. He was making a show of blocking in the marina.

"For an eight-by-ten?"

"Don't try to haggle for it. Buy three or more, you get twenty percent off."

It was a brisk evening with lots of traffic on the commercial lane. A street musician's impoverished guitar provided the soundtrack to matrons in military-style coats walking eastward toward the park hotels and girls in ridiculous high-fashion outfits prancing by on their way to cocktail hours. The painter watched the hems of their skirts as they passed, and even as I felt disgust for him I realized I had been doing the same. I drew up closer to watch him work. He was competent, of course. He painted quickly, each scene a repeat of a scene he'd done hundreds of times before. I was getting quick with my carving knife, though each image I did was new, and even though my pumpkins were admittedly not real artwork, I disliked the feeling of a parallel thread between me and this hat-wearing amateur.

"You sell many?"

"Summers? A ton. Fall and spring, enough. Wintertime I gotta play mall Santa."

"You're not even fat."

"Try and find a fat guy in Boston without an Irish accent."

He said he'd taken some community college classes before going to study with a few seascape painters up in Maine. He listed a few names I'd never heard of, names unknown outside the newspapers of the little communities they lived in, probably selling their paintings of marine rocks to the elderly via mail-order catalog. I told him to thin out his brushstrokes if he wanted to add more detail.

"I've been doing this for fifteen years, kid. I think I've got it down."

I figured he would be doing it fifteen more; in fact, I'd passed a sixty-year-old art hawker on my walk down Newbury whose paintings were nearly indistinguishable from these.

I gave him forty dollars. I had about two hundred with me, having deposited the nerve-wracking balance under my mattress at home. On my way back home from Back Bay, I stopped in a liquor store and spent most of the rest of what was in my pocket on a bottle of Paul Giraud. I had two leftover uncut pumpkins in my little studio, but the remaining eight I would need to bring home one by one, so I stopped next in a Back Bay grocery, though I could get them in Chinatown for half the price. The rest of the walk was a struggle, with the eight-by-ten tucked into the back of my jeans, a large pumpkin under my right arm, and my left hand wrapped around a bottle of the most expensive alcohol I'd ever bought, but I enjoyed the comic figure I cut as I waddled through downtown Boston like some overloaded Russian peasant.

There was no heater in my studio, but it was directly above the kitchen of the Vietnamese restaurant, and that heated my space quite well. Steam smelling of beef stock fogged through the gaps in the old hardwood flooring. I was obliged to do my carving, as well as my painting when I had time for it, in the corner by a window that I cracked open a few inches. It was the one place in the apartment I could keep cool, and I didn't want too much heat to set any of my carvings prematurely to rot.

I had just the key lines down: the bend of the river; the diagonal cut of the bridge; select trees along the bank; the squat outlines of the Back Bay condos; behind those, the tall silhouettes of the Pru and the Hancock tower. I set electronic tea lights inside them so I could see how the cavities would look illuminated, but I had to imagine the flicker, the movement, that actual candles would provide.

I kept a few fingers of cognac in my glass while I worked, and sipped at it when I stepped back to assess my progress. My carvings didn't typically require such a stock-taking, but I did so, outwardly, because this was a panorama, and one needed a little more distance to see the full scope. Inwardly, I did so because the rain-wet street outside the little window, the savory steam rising from below, and a glass of such a fine spirit were almost enough to make a pumpkin look like a work of art.

Deckinger called me at three thirty on Saturday, wanting to know if I was going to make his deadline. I told him I was putting the final touches on the last one and that I'd start hauling them up within the hour. I'd be bringing them one by one, I said, walking through the Common rather than taking the T, and each trip would take about twenty minutes.

I put aside what I'd actually been working on that morning: a new painting that had been occupying more and more of my brain-space since I'd stood in front of Deckinger's Durant. I always did my best work when I was neglecting something else important; I could channel the pressure of a deadline into an artificial deadline for myself.

Durant saw all the faces in the crowd, but my project was to see the crowd in a single face. I had a huge self-portrait going, divided into little rectangles like the index guides in an atlas. Eventually the guides would fade into the paint laid over them, but each little box would have distinctions both in a slightly different undertone and a slightly different cast of feature—that is, one corner of the mouth would be playfully smirking, the other turned down; one eye would appear to be the eye of a hero, the other the eye of an old woman on the subway. The trick was getting them to conspire to create one cohesive face, one only slightly fractured, able to draw the viewer closer to observe each panel and examine the infinite parallel versions of a single human countenance.

But that would all have to wait. I quickly fine-tuned the last of the pumpkins and stuck it under my arm. Outside, I was surprised to find a black car waiting for me, and a chauffeur holding a sign with my name on it as if I were being picked up at the airport. So I loaded all the pumpkins into the trunk, cushioning them with some Styrofoam blocks I had in my apartment, and we drove the short trip up the hill to Deckinger's condo.

The foyer looked the same, but the rooms beyond were decorated with framed posters for dozens of old horror movies: *Poltergeist*, *Rosemary's Baby*, *The Exorcist*, and so on. A rented bartender was setting up his table, and Deckinger sat on the corner of his sofa trying to connect his laptop to what seemed like a very complex stereo system. He was not impressed with the first pumpkin I brought in, decorated only with the tail of the river and a few trees. Nor was he happy when I told him I'd deviated from the specs he gave me, forgoing two rows of five pumpkins for a triangular design with just one pumpkin on the bottom left, rising to three high on the far right.

He studied the first one, his face looking something like a TV judge when he threatens to hold someone in contempt. That expression eased toward neutral as successive trips to the car filled in the tableau. The driver offered to help, but I would not have anyone else handling the delicate pieces. It took about fifteen minutes to come together. When they were all arranged Deckinger looked at me, shrugged, and said bemusedly, "What did I expect from pumpkins?" He counted out the balance of the commission from his wallet.

I wasn't worried. I took his money, crouched to a knee, and used long matches to light the eighty-two candles I had glued into position inside the cavities. I did the river first, in the foreground, and with only it and the silhouettes of trees illuminated it recalled the untouched landscape here before Boston. Then I lit the buildings, carefully carved with a pattern that showed certain offices still lit but others darkened for the night. For last I saved the lights of Fenway and the landmark Citgo sign on the right of the panorama. I had used cardboard cutouts and four different colors of candle for the Citgo sign so the triangle was separated into orange, red, and maroon just like on the sign itself, and the CITGO letters glowed blue and bold. Making it all come together had at first felt like I was fashioning the land with my hands, then like I myself had built the city on top of it, like I could conjure whole civilizations.

I stood back and observed it with Deckinger. Lights blinked on and off inside the buildings. The currents and eddies of the Charles moved and swirled in the magic of the candlelight. It was hard to believe this real bend in the Charles was just outside, less than a mile away, when it seemed to be living for the moment in this parlor. I looked over to Deckinger, but he didn't take his eyes off what I'd created.

He went to his kitchen and started polishing a lowball glass, which I think he did for show. He poured himself a dram of something darker than the cognac. There was no glass for me this time. "Well," he said. Then again, "Well. Isn't that fucking something?"

He got out his wallet again and counted out more cash, still watching the river dance. He'd tipped me five hundred dollars. Yet I found my own eyes now settled on his glass of that mystery spirit, thinking I might trade the whole tip for my own glass of it and for the name on the label.

In November I conferred with Professor Wei, and I found myself rushing through an explanation of my work—the painting I'd brought and the sketches I'd done for a few more—in order to tell him about Deckinger, his Durant, and my pumpkin-carving adventures. I lowballed the amount I made by several thousand—studio art professors brought in less than the cost of living in the Boston metro—and still I raised his eyebrows. I told him I had stumbled into a Beacon Hill client base, and he said, very pointedly, "A-ha."

My ideas for the Christmas season were still in development: intricate wire wreaths speckled with mirrors and candles; nativity or festivity mosaics; huge panels of holiday scenes constructed out of Christmas lights, like a Lite-Brite on crack, I said.

Professor Wei had an impressive slouch. His shoulder blades and sacrum were the only points of contact with his chair, his feet extended far in front of him, giving the impression that his body was the hypotenuse of a right triangle. It was more work, I was certain, than sitting straight up would have been. He did it when he was concentrating. He was also steepling his fingers, which signaled concentration squared.

"Hand me your sketchbook," he said. He flipped through it several times, taking so long on each page that I was sure he was preparing a scorching critique. The ambitious students flocked to his classes and the sensitive ones flocked away, for he was not one to mince words. In turn I began composing a mental apologia, though I never planned on using it, because while the professor never raised his voice, he never lost an argument either. When he finished he closed the book gently and slid it across the desk to me. He tapped the front and asked, "Why would you work on anything but this?"

Those were just ideas, I told him, ideas too derivative of Durant to be worth anything on their own. The carving had netted me my living expenses for most of a year, and hadn't even monopolized my time—half of this painting had been done during my busiest days of carving. If I could come up with another moneymaker for the holiday season, I could set myself up for the next two years and have half my student loans paid off by the time I graduated. Remembering the Jewish neighborhood down the street, I started extemporizing: artisan menorahs, micropainted dreidels. Only later did I realize how stupid this all sounded.

"But what you are talking about is craft, even if you are very good with these pumpkins. Tell me, how much would you pay for one of those?" He laughed. "I wouldn't buy one, no offense. I don't think you would, either. Not because they're not good for what they are, but because of what they are. Now tell me, how much would you pay for this Durant you saw?"

"I'm not talking about giving up painting."

"Did Evan Durant spend his time carving jack-o'-lanterns? A craftsman can schedule his time. An artist has to dive in. These are the best things I've seen in my classes in a long time."

At that hint of praise my argumentative tack dropped, and I lapsed into full-on therapy mode. I said maybe that was true, but what about the other classes at the school? What about all the classes at the handful of other art schools in Boston, or all the classes at the hundreds of schools across the nation? What about New York? What about people like Durant, who dropped out as undergraduates and painted under the radar for years? What about *time*, about multiplying the competition by each entering class of the future, filled with new prospects? Was it so bad to hedge my bets a little when some college dropout in a basement in Peoria was potentially doing the same thing I was doing but better?

I caught my breath and began to apologize. Professor Wei's slouch had intensified. He was staring up at the ceiling, and he looked like a plank that had been tipped over onto the office chair.

I wasn't sure his butt was even in contact with the seat cushion. He asked to see my notebook again, and I waited while he looked through it in much the same fashion as before.

"You're right about the odds. But you'll have your whole life to sell pumpkins to rich gentiles and menorahs to rich Jews if this doesn't pan out. As a professor my job is to spot talent and nurture potential, not to make any promises, but I will make you one promise regarding your potential: a friend of mine runs a gallery out in Brighton. If the rest of your series comes out as well as that one, I'll help you get your paintings in it."

So I forwent any holiday-themed business ventures and instead dove in, as Professor Wei had suggested, to the work. I had to start transporting the finished works to a storage closet at the school because there wasn't space in the unsteamed corner of my studio and I was worried about the canvases warping or taking on a beefy smell. A few times I asked the professor to take a look at them, but he refused, saying this was a personal project and I shouldn't let anyone else in just yet. He was right again. I had something I wanted to say to Durant: that I was not just one face in a crowd, that some people deserved to be the focus of their own painting. It was a personal project, and thus it was different than anything else I had created. Before I had always gauged my work by how closely it approximated the work of established masters and contemporary upstarts, but an internal metric had sprung out nowhere for these paintings, offering me intense joy when I felt I was hitting that shadowy goal and despair when I wasn't. When I couldn't get a detail right, I would feel the whole series was doomed.

I worked away through the coldest months. Snow was on the sidewalks and piled in the gutters outside, and little breezes blew the frigid air in through the little gap I left open at the window. I learned to calibrate it, two inches on cold days, one inch during the freezes, closed at 9 p.m., an hour before the kitchen below shut down. I imagined being interviewed one day in *Aesthetica* or *Juxta-*

poz and telling stories of my early days painting above a Vietnamese restaurant, drinking from a bottle of cognac I could not afford.

After the fragmented face I'd started in October, I worked on a crowd much like the ones in Durant's paintings, except every face in the crowd was my own, every expression a variety of expression I actually made. In another the faces of everyone in a crowd were blurred beyond recognition, except for one face (not mine—too obvious, of course) in high focus. I replicated the famous photo of Muhammad Ali towering over a downed Sonny Liston, but each of those faces in the background, those heads sticking up behind the ring, was Ali's as well, sharing his cock-headed moment of triumph, his dare to Liston to get up again. I became hyperaware of crowds when I was in public, aware of my place in them, whether I was dead center or on the fringes, where I would be if the crowd were composed and framed. I even sought some out: the game-day commuters at Kenmore, the new-exhibit-goers at the Museum of Fine Arts.

When May came, late in the semester, I had a twelve-painting series, and Professor Wei finally let me show it to him. We lined them up, five around the walls inside his office and the other seven in the hallway outside. He walked from piece to piece, examining each with his trademark silent-concentration face. It was not a good sign. In class he was effusive about the work he liked. He had sung Durant's praises for two hours, though no one in the class was interested. Watching him apply his critical eye made me reexamine the set from the perspective of an independent viewer, and the stress of his silence suffused me with doubts not about my technique but about my choices. I knew what he was going to say: the choices were wrong. The only portrait they showed was a self-centered pretender.

I realized I had never been taken apart before. I'd had no reviews in papers, little or big. My work had not been on any sites and had not been subject to angry comment threads. I'd exposed myself so far only within the womb of the academic workshop, where most of the students were middling and the professors paid to be gentle. As blunt as Professor Wei was in class, I sensed his workshop was a soft territory compared to where we were heading now.

He was steepling his fingers again, tapping the two index fingers together. When his response finally came, it was less thorough than I'd come in hoping for, but a much easier escape than I had been anticipating. "Well done," he said, and dialed a number on his cell phone.

"David, I have something to show you."

At that time I thought expectation was the hardest state, that I couldn't bear the waiting. When I think back to that summer, I remember doing a lot of walking around town. I'd walk north through the cobbled brick streets of Beacon Hill, cross the Longfellow Bridge into Cambridge, then cross the Harvard Bridge back to Back Bay. Other days I'd walk through the Fens and down to Jamaica Plain. My spurt of inspiration had played out, and I was eager for the next one to catch me, but so filled with ambition I was in no state to be caught. Halloween was around the corner, and I could once again bankroll the rest of the year, but I was reluctant to begin what Professor Wei had dismissed as craftwork when I had actual artwork hanging on the walls of that gallery out in Brighton. Only in retrospect can I see what a joy it should have been, feeling like I only had to choose what I wanted to become and it would happen.

On a Saturday in late September I took the T out to Brighton to begin collecting my paintings, none of which had sold. I was going to have to bring them back one by one and find a place to store them; I had graduated and no longer had access to the school facilities. I was an artist on my own now, and no one owed me anything. I'm sure the professor would have met with me to give me advice, but it was no longer his job, and I was embarrassed to visit him because it would have felt too much like begging. I went in and took the first canvas off its hooks, my self-portrait divided into every self I thought I could have been, my favorite to look at when I was composing them, the most painful to look at now.

Outside I leaned it against the wall to give Deckinger a call. I had a spreadsheet of all my clients from the previous year, and the plan was to start contacting them the first of October. I called Deckinger so early because he was my biggest ticket, but more so because I hoped he might buy one of my paintings, even if only out of nostalgia, even if only to have a story for his friends: "I bought this from the kid who carves my jack-o'-lanterns." If he only gave me eighty dollars for it, if he hung it in his walk-in closet, the sale would mean more to me than another five thousand dollar commission.

He answered, and I told him who was calling.

"Never heard of you," he said.

I repeated my name and reminded him of the pumpkins from last year. "That's right," he said. "They were a big hit. Everybody loved it. Thought you should know. It's the way the world works, right? You pay an artist for work in your home and manage to steal all the credit."

"I don't need the credit," I said. "I'm glad they went off well."

I told him about my ideas for his pumpkins this year, that I could do a Sistine Chapel that would blow his mind, or a crowd of horror-movie villains. Sales weren't in my blood, but I thought I was coming on smooth. I was aiming for bigger spreads, more pumpkins, more cash in my pocket.

"I haven't thought much about what I'm doing this year, but when I do I'll have my secretary get in touch. Look, I'm getting on the bridge. I've got to go." He hung up before I could renew my pitch. From that point on, I knew the score. I knew there would be no call from any secretary. I even knew Durant no longer graced his foyer, now that Guy Bonner was the soup du jour. I took my painting and got on the train.

In Allston, though, I had to get off because the train became too crowded. At each stop, at the usually empty stops after the line turned left off Commonwealth, new people poured on. What had been a ghost train in Brighton was now full of elbows that did not bode well for my canvas. At Packard's Corner I made the decision to walk the rest of the way. It would take a lot longer to bring home all the paintings this way, but it was a walk I enjoyed, down Commonwealth right in front of Boston University, with the river peeking from behind in the gaps between buildings.

At first I'd been unable to figure out what drew the crowd that day. It was too early in the morning for a Red Sox game, too early in the week for the Patriots. Even in the "Athens of America," as a few old-fashioned folks still called Boston, plays and museum openings didn't draw like this. The traffic was backed up as well, at a complete standstill in the eastbound lanes and not much better westbound, and even the sidewalks were overwhelmed with a mix of the young and old.

When I got closer to the center of campus I saw pavilion tents and young women in scarlet polos ushering about young people in backpacks. It was Boston University's move-in day, and four thousand new students were swarming east Allston with their parents in tow. There was music playing; there were games, festivities, booths, all signaling the commencement of a new age and new possibilities for the arriving students. Along the street, buskers and artists had come to take their tithe, selling Citgo signs and Fenway Parks and paintings of the Common. I even saw the street artist—the one who'd sold me the panorama for Deckinger's pumpkins that day in Back Bay—hauling in hundreds with his infinitely replaceable work.

I leaned my painting against a garbage can and walked on without it. It could decorate a dorm room or migrate to the dump, but that was no longer my concern. As I trekked farther up Commonwealth, I saw what was stopping traffic. A clumsy U-Haul driver had driven his truck through an underpass without enough clearance, shearing off half of the overhead storage compartment and wedging the vehicle in so tightly that two parallel tow trucks were trying to pull it out together. A piece of wooden furniture too mangled to identify lay along the line between lanes, surrounded by a smashed TV and scattered boots and dresses. A girl in a tube top berated her father on the sidewalk. The foot traffic swarmed around it all and walked on unaffected, and the subway cars rattled by, and the river flowed on as always.

At home I poured myself a small glass of Paul Giraud and drank it slowly. I had a few inches left in the bottom of the bottle, and when I was done I hid it away in the back of a cabinet and never touched it again, because I know that when it's gone, it's gone.

THE LAW OF THREES

They roll out at 10 p.m. with the radio crackling. Whit tries to keep his mind on the LSAT study books hidden in the book bag at his feet. The messages coming through the speaker urge everyone to be careful, to exercise caution, but the whole night-shift fleet is swirling around the parking lot like a cloud of energized bees. In the hallways of the station, the mood had been somber, almost silent. It was amazing to see grown, armed men feel so vulnerable in the guarded hallways of their own station. But now that each pair is wrapped in a cruiser, some doing donuts or fishtailing out of figure eights, the lot is a rave of red and blue lights. The men roll past Whit and Vargas flashing three fingers in the air, expecting to see them flashed back. Whit does not lift his hand. Though he's always had the tendency to be carved by the expectations of others, he won't celebrate this. He remembers this mood. High school. Homecoming. The radio says *stay safe out there*, but the body politic says *be aggressive, B-E aggressive*.

Vargas rolls out plenty slow, the caboose of the train, steering with his elbows while he eats his nightly cup of chocolate pudding. He regards himself as some kind of sage or oracle, and Whit supposes anyone who's been patrolling so long without being promoted out of it has to. He waxes his mustache, not with a hipster twirl but into a fat black slug that overfills the entire upper lip. Somehow he never gets his pudding in it, which does indeed feel like a mystical power. Vargas also thinks there's power in moving slowly. Whit is not sure there's power in anything the force does. But other times he thinks every one of his actions is a wasted act of power: resting a hand on a holster, speeding down an empty night street, or even stopping on a busy sidewalk to double-knot a loosened shoelace.

When the cars come out of the lot, they split left and right into two trails, and from there into smaller and smaller groups until finally he and Vargas are alone headed southwest on International. You can smell the canal and the marshy coastline a few blocks away. The smell travels farther at night, a stink of plant matter ripening in still water. A few blocks more and they're in what Vargas calls Zombieland: weak, irregular streetlamps illuminating now and then the dead souls pushing shopping carts full of obsolete VCRs, or walking that slow junkie waltz with the whole body rocking. Then there are the groups, the gangs, three or four or five teens walking abreast in the street, enlarged by their oversize athletic apparel. If there's a pipe being passed or a gun tucked in the back of a belt, or anything else citable, Vargas likes to startle them with the lights and siren and watch them scurry, he says, like bugs.

Whit's foot nudges his satchel, heavy with two fat books of practice questions.

"You know what the people who live here call it?" he asks Vargas. This would have been a good retort if he'd said it months ago, when Vargas had first claimed the naming rights. He's thought of the word often since, but not until tonight has it seemed important to point out. Vargas raises his eyebrows, waiting to be amused.

"Home," he says.

"Not as catchy."

They pass a bum toting an out-of-season Christmas tree over his shoulder, nearly dragging a soggy-hipped basset hound behind him; a ten-year-old weaving down the street on a bicycle with a basket full of groceries; a donut shop they both choose not to mention tonight, the only lit storefront on an avenue composed of security-gated laundries, vacuum repair shops, ethnic groceries, and massage brothels.

"Besides," Vargas says, "you're assuming their view from the inside is more accurate than ours from the outside. Those uncontacted tribes in the Amazon—you think they can see themselves more clearly than we can? You think you see yourself more clearly than I do? You think those law books say the same thing to me?"

Vargas has dropped hints before that he knew what was in Whit's bag, but this is his first direct statement about it. Whit has broken new ground, perhaps, with his challenge to the Zombieland moniker. The exchange feels, in a sad way, like something that could pass for closeness.

"What do my books say?" he asks.

"My mother taught me about when you can't say anything nice."

At eleven thirty, they see a kid holding ground on a known corner. Vargas tells Whit to shake him up a bit and parks across the street, where he has a good line of sight.

"Be safe," he calls as Whit gets out of the car. "Exercise caution."

Whit walks over to the darkened corner: a minimart porched by a single concrete step, on which the kid stands, leaning back against the crosshatching of the door gate. He's a teen, by his size, but more is hard to tell given the scrawny, loose-limbed body and the incongruous baby-fatted face. Whit shows his badge and says his name. The kid says nothing. Whit asks his name. He says it's Gino.

"Isn't that an Italian name?"

"Holoman," Gino says. "Isn't that kind of mayonnaise?"

Whit's always been able to feel it when he blushes: a girlish warmth that hits the neck as much as the cheeks. He smirks through it. It was a good line. Whit wants to show the kid he can laugh at himself without giving away authority, that he's not one of the brutes who'll slam Gino's head into a wall for a stray word. Someday Whit will need honest information, and this decency, this showing of humanity, will pay dividends. Though if his test prep course is worth its ridiculous sticker price, he might not be around to see it. But that damn blush—it flushes any authority down the toilet.

"You know how it works," he tells Gino. The kid puts his hands against the wall. Whit pats him down: his ribs, his back, his moist armpits, the back and front of his belt, where they like to keep their guns, though corner kids get frisked enough they usually know better. His ankles, calves, knees, thighs. Whit pats the outsides of his oversize pockets. It can be hard to feel anything but pills in there—he's missed things before, been razzed for it by the most asinine of street cops—so he reaches into Gino's pockets to check for powders, weed, money, scraps of paper with phone numbers penciled on them. There's nothing, as he expected. The stash will be hidden nearby. But he has to check, they say: if you don't catch the dumb ones you won't catch any. He brushes something soft through the fabric of the pocket, and his hand startles back.

"Buy me a drink first?" Gino says.

"A real comedian," he says. He digs an elbow into the kid's back, the way he remembers his own older brother doing when he pinned Whit down as a kid, an unbearable pressure against the ribs. But since there's plenty of space between Gino and the wall, there's too much give to cause him any discomfort.

"Shiatsu," he says. "Hot stone."

"Go home," Whit tells him. Whatever lookout he might have has scooted off. "What kind of mother lets her kid out at this hour?" The kid does a little dance, snapping his fingers above his shoulders at Whit. Then he does a twirl and slides off.

Vargas chuckles as Whit climbs back into the cab, and Whit goes hot in the neck again. Vargas says he'll tell the boys Whit tried. "But off the record," he says, "you'll never outclown a kid with no bank account. What they lack in material assets they make up in cheap irony. You can't smooth talk them, kid. They only love the boot." He sees the look Whit gives him, and offers back a mockery of his piety. "It's not racist. I came up around here."

Aimless driving. They take a call for a toddler having febrile seizures, and stand around in the wet night air while the paramedics do their thing. A noise complaint: lovers' quarrel, a woman in a bathrobe holding a cheese grater like it's a deadly weapon. No B&E from dispatch, though, no gunshots lodging in the studs of apartment walls, no carjackings. At 1:13 a.m. a howl comes in not from dispatch but from another black-and-white: responding to apparent burglary at Weston and Campbell, broken storefront glass, young black male seen nearby with a suspicious backpack. It doesn't make sense: that intersection is just a bail bondsman and an electronics repair shop; why rob a place where everything is broken? At 1:18 another call comes through with a little more octane on it: shots fired at Campbell and Booth, officers unharmed, suspect down. Whit's stomach lurches. And Vargas has that slow way about him, and his mouth half hidden by that baby-shit mustache, and Whit can't tell at all what that expression means. Regret, amusement, resignation, righteousness? Is it giving him too much credit to say he sighs when he responds?

"Well," he says, unreadable. "That's one."

Whit had thought it was all bluster and bluff. How could it be otherwise? That thought: this can't be the world. As though Vargas can see the kind of spiral Whit is headed down—forehead against the cold window, mouth gone mute—he pulls into a Denny's parking lot and tells Whit he has no choice about getting a cup of coffee. Whit goes along. He wants off the street. The counter waitress is Joan, but just the N on her nametag has turned sideways so it reads JOAZ. This is all Vargas calls her, flirting in a way she clearly wants nothing to do with. He pours so much cream and sugar into his coffee it's like he's trying to make another cup of pudding.

"You've got to keep your imagination in the right place," he says. "Whalen's fiancée curled sideways on the least comfortable of ICU recliners while all those monitors beep away like fucking R2-D2. Waking up to see his face interrupted by a ventilator tube. Nguyen's wife. Think of her awake right now, middle of the night, knowing that tomorrow she's going to get a dozen visits from people she can barely understand. A guy like Nguyen probably had thirteen kids that all live off the rice noodles his paycheck afforded. Tomorrow her house is going to look like a florist's wet dream, but she's only going to be able to think about the dwindling sack of rice in the pantry."

"Mercy," Whit says. Vargas clearly doesn't know what he means, and neither does Whit, but Vargas stops.

"Tell me about this test, then. You have to know all the laws?"

"That's the bar. This is just a test of logic." Whit tells him about the three sections: reading comprehension, logical reasoning, logic games. The games are the hardest, at least at first—full of weird scenarios governed by weird rules. Six students are each going to see one of four movies. Three canoes with four seats each, and each canoe needs one adult and three children. Who is the best tennis player? If G plays golf, he's the worst tennis player, but if he doesn't, he's the third best. But it's the most learnable section—at least that's what his teacher, barely more than a kid in fancy threads and glasses, promises every class. So far, yes, the games make more sense if he spends an hour on one, but when he tries to get through four in the thirty-five minutes the test gives him, it's like trying to read computer code. That's not what he tells Vargas. He tells him there are four game types, and each one has its own sketch. He explains, as best he can, how to form the contrapositive to a conditional statement. He finds himself cribbing words from his instructor's lectures pretty much verbatim, but he sounds confident. It occurs to him that this is what Vargas was going for: getting his brain into a sphere where it's more comfortable. He doesn't mind the manipulation. He keeps going even when Vargas's eyes glaze over.

The radio vibrates on the counter next Vargas's side of bacon, calling out something about a suspicious young black ma—Vargas turns the dial off, signs the check with *To Joaz my one true love* and his phone number, and motions Whit back to the car. He turns the radio back on when the doors are safely shut and locked, but there's no chatter, nothing to indicate the count has gotten any closer to its terminus, and Whit discovers something about himself: he wanted the awful thing to be over so much that a part of him had wished for it to happen.

He wants so badly to throw up that he rolls the window down and sticks his head out, but what's in his stomach won't fit through his throat. They're farther south now, and farther inland. The air has lost its mossy smell. Now it's just the day's exhaust. Looking out through the blank night air he sees scattered big luxurious windows of the hillside houses lit up from the inside, insomniacs with their cable televisions on. They don't need to worry about rising sea levels up there, but Whit remembers—he was a kid, but he remembers—when the whole range lit up like a quick-burning log in 1991, and three thousand houses dissolved into crackling black paper.

Cops up there give warnings if champagne parties go too loud too late. Cops up there make sure no one up there is from down here.

The dead streets quiver with a useless electricity. There's no squeal of street-racing tires, no thumping of steroidal subwoofers, no rattle of shopping cart casters or calls of birds or even the grapey hiccupping of crickets. Engine noise and an open window. Vargas never runs the radio, neither music nor talk, and the squad radio has gone so quiet Whit imagines some sort of dread cloud hanging over the city soaking up all transmissions. He feels alone in the world.

Vargas rolls up Whit's window from his armrest, and its cool slate catches the skin of his forehead and lifts it upward. Vargas's posture is stiff as a startled deer's, and he's looking past Whit, out the passenger window down Fremont, and Whit follows the tether of his gaze to the crew of seven marching down the middle of the street, and there's no word for it but marching. This is a mission, not a stroll. They are headed south toward norteño territory. Something bad is going to happen. Vargas coasts to a stop. Thirty seconds later Whit's watching them through the windshield, twenty feet in front of the bumper. They eye the squad car skeptically but keep moving. Whit waits for Vargas's hand to go to the PA.

"Don't get crazy," Vargas says. "I'm not putting money on a two-on-seven game of basketball."

"This is our job," Whit says.

"They do our job for us."

"Kids get killed in their beds. Stray bullets."

"Anecdotal."

Whit wants to spit in his face. Vargas's eyes narrow. He asks: "Has anyone ever told you that when you get pissy, your mouth looks like a butthole?" He puts the car back in gear, and they creep north, opposite from where the crew was headed. Driving back that way, back in the direction of downtown, of the bridge, of the ghost silhouette of a more civilized city, he no longer feels alone in the world. He feels crowded in the car. His hands itch. His face itches. He tries to check his imagination, as his partner has recommended. He sees Mrs. Nguyen in front of a casket. He sees Whalen's fiancée, and Whalen sedated and intubated on the table, breathing that robot breath, the rise and fall of his ribs too perfect, too regular. He can't help but see as well the possibility of a line going flat and half a dozen nurses rushing into the room and setting to work with a defibrillator. He can't help but see that possibility of them shocking only dead flesh that bounces, rubbery, but won't come back. The possibility that with two dead cops, the law of threes will demand six.

Ten minutes later, the radio crackles. A gunfight between gangs, not far south of where they just were, broke up on its own with no casualties. Vargas smirks. One of his great amusements is how gangbangers who love to pose tough with their guns have no idea how to aim them. But the smirk disappears into teeth as he chews his bottom lip. Perhaps he's remembered that the 11th Street Boys who gunned down Whalen and Nguyen figured it out well enough. Dispatch wants a car to respond and set up a crime scene. Vargas calls in cross streets four miles north of their actual location and asks if they want him to head down. They decline. Closer cars, they say.

He finally reaches a half-decent neighborhood and parks under the lights of a twenty-four-hour grocery. "We should while away some time," he says. "Get in a better headspace." He does this on nights when he doesn't want to get mixed up in anything that might result in paperwork. He calls it his special union break. Tonight, he's got a story to tell. His wife went snooping through his oldest son's closet this last weekend and found a stash that would have garnered their captain a press conference: a two-and-a-half-foot water bong, half an ounce of weed, ultra-sensitive condoms, and a travel-size shampoo bottle filled with olive oil—Whit will never guess what the olive oil was for, Vargas says, or maybe he will. Whit tunes him out. Vargas doesn't remember telling him the exact same story in May.

Whit closes his eyes and thinks: evidence, conclusion, assumption. Logical flaw. Parallel reasoning. Method of argument. The quietest times his mind has had in months have been during the practice tests he's taken: perfect silence, the timer set for thirty-five minutes per section, with one question in front of him to be dispatched, and then the next. He wonders if they can spend the rest of the shift like this: camped out. Hiding out. If Vargas relaxes into a certain mood Whit might even be able to crack open the books.

But of course that's a dream. Just after 3:30 a.m., the radio sparks to life again.

Is it possible to go crazy in the span of five hours? Whit's mind keeps heating up until he thinks it will catch flame, then going blank and cold. He presses the button to roll down the window. Nothing happens. Vargas has the child lock on it. Whit tells him to roll down the window. Vargas tells him to calm down. "Roll down the fucking window," Whit shouts. Vargas rolls it down halfway.

After the last radio call, Vargas said he wanted to get a damn donut. His eyes have reddened, and the sacks under them are puffy. It's wearing on him too, Whit thinks, but not enough to exculpate him. They're headed back north on a main avenue, and it feels like coming out of the depths, like coming up from a dive, even as Whit's mind tangles itself with red thread. He's thought already about all the things he could do: call someone at the *Tribune*; go through the upper brass; document, document, document. These options all seem to have the weight of impossibility on them. But they don't, he knows, and that doesn't absolve him. They are all logistically simple. The impossibility is inside of himself.

As they pass back through Zombieland every soul they see is haunted in Whit's mind by an officer with his pistol to the back of his head, and none of them has the slightest idea. There are fewer out now, few for whom 4 a.m. isn't either too early or too late. They see the same bum sleeping next to his Christmas tree on the sidewalk, his basset hound using his thigh as a pillow. A few early bread trucks are out, something that's always seemed out of place here, a relic of a charming old New York or Chicago, rather than this stripped-down urban wasteland. The lumberyard is closed, but under the security lights it looks like a dinosaur graveyard, and Whit watches one tired security guard patrolling the aisles.

"What's that kid's name?" Vargas asks. He's keeping pace with a kid strolling on the right-hand sidewalk. Whit recognizes him.

"Gino."

Vargas rolls Whit's window the rest of the way down. "Go home, Gino," he calls across Whit.

Gino stops and smirks at them. "Who's Gino?" he asks. "My name's Melvin."

"Whatever the fuck your name is," Vargas says, "you should go home."

"Thanks, Mom. I mean ma'am. I mean officer."

Vargas chuckles. If Whit knows him at all, he's about to kneel on the kid's back and cite him for something stupid and hard to dodge: urinating on a public building; graffiti; indecent exposure. Vargas is a turtle, but he can be a snapping turtle. But his voice shifts into a sincere register Whit hasn't even heard him use to talk about his own kids.

"Trust me, kid. You want to be at home tonight."

The kid is suspicious of his tone, but he shrugs and says he will, before starting up a slower stroll in the same direction. Vargas gets rolling again, and Whit watches the kid shrink away in his side mirror. Who cares? Donuts and coffee are only a few blocks away. Fuck the cliché. It's two hours to sunrise, and Whit has been up since 5 p.m. yesterday. A long time ago in a galaxy far, far away.

Vargas makes a pudding of his coffee again. Whit puts in a hint of milk and about five grains of sugar. Vargas: a jelly donut and a maple bar. Whit: an apple fritter. Whit's almost disappointed he won't be around long enough to see Vargas develop the insulin routine he's going to need in a few years. Whit's been looking at schools nearby, and in a fifty-mile radius he's got two reach schools, four safety schools, and a few in between, but he's starting to see the virtue in distant kingdoms: Northwestern in foggy Chicago, Tulane in dirty New Orleans, Notre Dame tucked away in the corn.

"The question I'm keeping myself sane with," Vargas says, "is 'does it matter?' Does it affect the situation in Egypt or Hong Kong? Does it drop more people into poverty? Does it sadden the nation?"

"Does it need to?"

"If you zoom out a little, three isn't that much."

"Jesus."

"From a cosmic perspective."

"Jesus fucking christ."

Whit sits in silence. But this logic is viral. He feels it wiggling like a worm in his brain. It's not rare to see a hundred or more violent deaths a year. Three in a week barely registers as an outlier. It is true: no one will be upset but a few stray family members. A part of Whit's mind is telescoping out like a rising shot in a film, showing him a broader scope of land outside of which this quake won't even register. For just a moment he wants to pull out his gun and put two into Vargas's chest as he sits on that cheap plastic bench licking jelly off his lower lip. Unwilled, he imagines himself doing it.

Is it possible to go crazy in the span of five hours?

Whit closes his eyes, and again, he sees himself doing it: stand, draw, bang, bang.

He rises and bursts through the door of the donut shop into the bracing air. It takes him a moment to decipher what he sees: a statue five feet away from the open window of the squad car, letting loose an upward arc of urine through the open passenger window. Of course it's no statue, though he stands remarkably still, with his hips arched forward like those cupids, and the stream has an impressive constancy. It's Gino. It's Melvin. Who knows what it says on his social security card?

Never afterward does he remember covering the fifteen feet between the shop door and the parking lot. Never afterward does he remember the tackle. It all happens like those rare, glorious moments he used to have on the wrestling mat, when his body moved perfectly without the brain's approval—and suddenly he's there: Gino's on his back, and Whit's elbow presses into his cheek, pinning his head to the ground, and Whit's gun is in his hand, the muzzle against Gino's temple. He'll always remember it as someone else, someone with a voice the twin of his own, saying: "You little shit. Don't you know what tonight is?" What he will remember, always, is looking into Gino's eyes, waiting for the fear, needing to see the fear, but seeing none. He will remember Gino staring up at him with empty, empty eyes, and the realization, like being born, that the kid knew exactly what tonight was. That he'd always known what tonight was. That he'd known his whole life.

THE TOP OF FRESNO

Sunsets from Apogee were not particularly impressive. The coastal range was so far west and so gentle, and so much smog hung in the intervening distance, that you couldn't see the mountains. The sun, rather than truly setting, seemed to just get blurry and dim and then fade away. Nor was the view after dark any more exciting. None of the other towers in town were as tall as the old Fresno Bank Building, atop which our restaurant, perched like a kitsch flying saucer, slowly rotated. Several of the other skyscrapers were abandoned, and only the hospital was fully lit in the nighttime. The streetlights uptown were too distant and regular to be inspiring. The poorer neighborhoods nearby reminded us of their plight through their dimness. So when Iris called me at ten thirty on my Saturday off to let me know the rotator gears were filling the restaurant with the smell of raw tires and she'd had to shut the motor off, I didn't jump out of bed.

She launched into her updates as soon as I picked up the phone, so I was able to act like her call had woken me up. "You need me to come fix it tonight?"

"For these old hats? I've been dosing out so much free sherry they think we're still spinning."

"I'll check it out in the morning."

It wasn't too much to worry about, she said: the Bulldogs were playing, and it had been quiet for a Saturday. The customers didn't mind, or didn't let on. Most of the people there were boosters, like her, and in a place with as few boosters as Fresno that meant they were all her friends. None were there for the novelty of a changing view. The motive common among them was pity, either for her or for themselves. I'd gone in for payroll paperwork that afternoon and knew the slender blue dress she was wearing. I could picture her, pulling out a chair from a two-top in the unoccupied side of the dining room, using one hand to hold her phone to her ear and the other to pick up a thin vase and smell the mums. This time of night, especially with something the matter, she'd have a port glass or a champagne flute, but she would be sipping slowly. She drank enough to make her regrets feel poetic, and no more.

"Is that *your* bed you're sleeping in, Nick? Dee called in sick tonight."

Dee was one of the waitstaff. I was tempted to tell Iris I kept my dick out of the restaurant, but that had a charge I didn't want to add to the conversation. I mumbled instead that it was my bed, and Dee had probably called in because of her boyfriend's gig at Tokyo Garden. I visualized receiving dental anesthesia, trying to get more sleep in my voice, though I knew it would do nothing to rush her off the phone. I wasn't sure whether I wanted to talk to her. I wasn't sure if she was flirting, wasn't sure if I wanted her to be. "Not sure" was something of a mantra for me at the time, a blank check I refused to fill in.

"Frank there?" I asked, hoping the invocation of her husband would sober the chat.

"Football game. The sedative effects of warm Coors."

I let a silence hang, considering a fake snore.

"It's a clear night," she said. "I'm not sure why. If you lean against the windows and look up, you can see the constellations."

"Good thing this happened after dark. Send smoke out the top of the building before sunset and you'll have pictures all over the web."

"The gators." This is what she called the Fresno residents who loved to disparage the city. It sounded more mature than haters.

"The gators," I said.

"Sounds like you're waking up," she said. "You sure you don't want to come in tonight?"

Our conversation would be much the same if I were there. Though probably bawdier, more direct. Restaurant talk. This was the hour of coffee and port, mousse and Black Forest cake. The late-stayers talked from table to table. The men watched Iris's hips as she strolled her territory. She was in her forties, and looked her age, but no less good for it. This late, she let the seams of the restaurant show: Lupe playing Lola Beltrán loud enough to be heard in the dining room while she scrubbed down the kitchen; young bussers without their aprons, their top buttons undone; plates, still steaming from the dishwasher, clanking as they were piled at the salad station. Iris conveyed the sense that this was the hour she was most herself, a self that was both elusive and present. Her plaintiveness made her sexy. I wanted to think that she did this out of instinct—that she didn't know why, but that I, with a male intuition, discerned the unconscious allure: a chance to satisfy the unsatisfied—but I was fairly certain she knew exactly what she was doing. What was it, then, that tamed our conversation? The presence of witnesses, maybe, but more the understanding that the promises she made when she was too nakedly herself would fade away as quickly as the impressions made on your skin by a pillow. In person, the context was clear. On the phone we were just one voice against another, wide open.

"Night, Iris," I said, knowing she would appreciate the spirit of an abrupt goodbye.

"Sweet dreams," she said, squeezing the words in just before I ended the call.

I preferred to come in early despite, or perhaps because of, the fact that I rarely had reason to. The sunrises from Apogee actually had something to them. I arrived Sunday morning in time to see a red ball squeezing up between the snowcaps of the Sierra Nevadas. Rain a few days ago had turned the sky blue again, brilliant blue above the soup of colors spilling out over the tops of the mountains. The restaurant was beautifully quiet. The repetitive sound of a wire brush scouring mussels in the kitchen was its own kind of silence. Our chef, Lupe, and her husband Phil liked to shop and prep early and take the midday off. We couldn't support a lunch service on the weekends. Iris had tried to establish a Sunday brunch, but all the brunch people lived ten miles north in the sprawl. The sprawl, the sprawl—Iris hated the sprawl. Sprawl is what happens, she said, when you have a city no one wants to be a part of.

Just standing there, facing east, I somehow made enough noise to be heard from the kitchen. "What you looking at, Nick?" I heard Phil shout.

"The sprawl," I said.

"The sprawl, the sprawl," Lupe said. "All full of the gators."

In the kitchen, Phil was hulling strawberries while Lupe took the beards off the mussels. They offered me eggs. I said I'd had cereal. "You insult the chef," Lupe said. It was a sort of routine, comforting as a rerun.

"Iris safe to drive last night?"

"Frank picked her up," Lupe said.

"Even though he was less safe," Phil added.

The access hatch for the machine room was in the middle of the kitchen. I had to move pots out of the way and crawl through some open shelving to get to it. As assistant manager, I had become the de facto mechanic as well. There are only a few real mechanics in the country who do this kind of work, and their travel costs, let alone the specialty fees, run to the ridiculous. Technologically, a rotating restaurant isn't much more than a huge lazy Susan with a motor to turn it. Tending the machinery usually just meant changing the oil and tightening some bolts that tended to vibrate loose. Occasionally it meant scouring the web for diagrams and message boards that contained the information I needed. Twice I'd tried calling the Top of Waikiki, who'd sold us the restaurant structure and its associated machinery, only to be brusquely reminded that they were the busiest restaurant on Oahu and the auction had not included consultations.

Climbing down the ladder offered some of the pleasures of descending into a submarine, even if it was only a half story down to a crawl space. The skunky, rubbery smell lingering down there actually enhanced those pleasures. After scooting on my back to the motor, I did the few things I knew: changed the oil, though what was in there wasn't too dark; cleaned the rotator belt; removed and cleaned the contact plate. Meanwhile, the sound of non-rubber soles started clacking from the surface above me. The vibrations shivered through the metal framing of the crawl space. When I'd finished my maintenance, I flipped the local start lever. The motor farted some black musk in my face.

"Hasn't had anything?" I heard Iris saying as I returned to the bottom of the ladder. She was talking with her mouth full. "If you make it, he's not going to turn it down."

After washing my face, I sat down across from her and her plate of steak and eggs. I could hear and smell my steak searing in a pan. I hadn't been sure I wanted breakfast, but now I knew I did. Iris was holding the steak in her hand to eat it, as if it were a crust of bread, but she managed to do so without looking like a barbarian. She used a corner of it to pop an egg yolk.

"Well?" she asked.

"Beyond my powers."

"Call Waikiki?"

"Assholes."

"Well, shit," she said. She stirred her yolk with a fingertip. Behind her, Phil gagged with indeterminate authenticity. "Give me a few minutes." She fished her phone from her purse and took it out to the dining room, still holding her steak in her other hand. That's when I noticed she was wearing the same blue dress from the night before, and that in places it was rumpled. This immediately enraptured me at the same time it put a knot of discomfort in my gut. I pictured her nudging her high heel off with her bare opposite foot and collapsing on her comforter, saw the light creases in the exposed backs of her knees. I saw her getting up in the morning next to a hairy-backed mound of snoring husband, tugging her hem down, and washing off yesterday's mascara. It felt, more than anything, like the dirty excitement of stumbling in on her changing.

She returned, saying she'd talked to some friends at Overlook in San Francisco, and that if we went up tonight they could give me a tutorial and even some spare parts. "We?" I said. "You've got to keep the restaurant open."

She checked something on her phone. "Twelve in the reservation book. So probably, what, twenty, all night? You realize that's a loss."

"We've already done half the prep," Phil said, laying his knife on the countertop.

"Paid holiday," she said. "You really want to complain?" Lupe wiggled her eyebrows at Phil. Then, holding my gaze, Iris said, "Come on. It'll be fun."

Lupe and Phil looked at each other, and then at me, as if this were a terribly ill-advised offer. If they hadn't, I don't think I would have accepted.

We left Fresno in a car that fit only the two of us. Her Mercedes felt like a whole different animal than my old GMC, a thoroughbred compared to a mule. I was driving so she could cancel the night's reservations, and, I suspect, so she could watch me enjoy it. As we burned up the 99 and then west to Los Banos, I prayed all the highway patrol officers were still in church. Meanwhile, Iris chatted for twenty minutes with everyone from the list. They were all regulars, all the heart of a struggling downtown revitalization effort. Most of them owned their own hip but unprofitable businesses there and benefited from the circle of support. The mayor was on the list too, and the president of the junior college. I imagined they would feel relief at their Sunday off, and pictured them secretly, guiltily chowing down at the Olive Garden in the eastern sprawl. At the end of all those calls, she had one more to make.

"Frank," she said. "The rotator is broken, and I've got to head to San Francisco for some parts"—"no, closing for the night"—"yes, big trails of black smoke; turn it on during the day and we'd have pictures all over the web"—"honey, you can't just turn an escalator into stairs"—"tonight, but probably late." The voice she used with him sounded like something out of musical theater. She signed off with kisses and closed her phone.

"In that case, he'll play an extra round of golf."

Frank was one of the developers building predesigned lofts downtown. Rather than actually converting the abandoned industrial spaces we had, they were pouring and sealing new concrete-floored apartments with exposed ducts and piping. But his actual money was from new housing tracts on the outskirts of town in all cardinal directions, projects that were still ongoing, continually increasing the sprawl, the sprawl. Iris surely knew all this, but she never revealed whether she'd found the penance of his downtown investments, including the restaurant, adequate, and I had my suspicions. Like many wealthy men, he indulged the artistic fancies of his wife, though her art was in trying to make Fresno a genuine city. Like most people accepting patronage, she could not help resenting it.

As we passed some invisible boundary, the smell of a dairy infused the car.

"Thank God we've got the top up," I said, "though I'm not sure how much difference it makes."

"I kind of like it. It's an authentic smell."

"Authentic cow shit."

"I like lots of bad smells. Skunk, old fruit."

"How about the smell our rotator is making?"

"No. No burn smells. That's human, inauthentic."

"By that logic, your restaurant smells worse than a dairy."

I didn't mean for this to come out barbed, but it did. I could tell I'd wounded her, and she looked away for a minute before she responded.

"Did you know that revolving restaurants are completely out of style? Before us, the last time one opened in the US was 1996. Top of Waikiki got a new one because Hawaii is time-locked. Blended drinks, cocktail umbrellas, floral print. Style doesn't matter." I told her I didn't know how much it mattered in Fresno, either. We might not be time-locked, but we were so far behind the times we might as well be. Trends migrated to Fresno like poor retirees. I was trying to be conciliatory, to make the case for Apogee fitting Fresno, but her expression made it clear how badly my attempt was going.

"It's lonely, isn't it?" I asked. "Believing in Fresno, believing that you can change its vision of itself."

She put her hand on my leg.

"Sure it's lonely," she said. "What isn't?"

She had me there.

We sped along the highway like bandits until the traffic in San Jose stopped us cold. Iris was able to get out and fold the top down in the middle of the carpool lane. This kind of gridlock on a Sunday afternoon was a bit bewildering. In Fresno, the only Sunday traffic happened in clusters around the bigger churches at 9 and 10 a.m. Things were different, I surmised, when you had a place people wanted to go. Creeping up the peninsula like that, half a mile at a time, should have been excruciating. In places where the freeway paralleled pedestrian paths, we could only watch with envy as people walking their dogs outpaced us. But here on the coast, we didn't need speed to get the wind in our hair. The sun was warm. The air was cool, and it had a bit of the ocean in it. We could see out to the bay, see the little triangles of windsurfers drifting across the dark water. Being stopped for all this was just fine.

She'd asked me earlier what wasn't lonely.

I thought, but didn't say: this isn't.

* * *

The woman who greeted us at Overlook wore aggressive bangs and a dress that probably cost a month's rent. She seemed to be one of those people who only exist in the great cities, with the looks of a model, the style of the rich, the unblinking attitude of the young. Though my age or younger, she was the general manager of a glitzy restaurant in a cultural capital, a person whose résumé you imagined printed in gold ink. She introduced herself as Cherise. From the way she and Iris shook hands, it was clear that this friend wanting to help her out was actually a stranger on the other end of a business transaction.

We'd ridden up in glass elevators, looking out over the garden atrium of a twenty-story luxury hotel. The restaurant was no less impressive, with a glittering granite front desk, hanging light fixtures that must have been individually polished, and a dining space that even with twice the tables we had seemed less cluttered.

"Look how beautiful it all is," Iris said. "If I had a whole staff like Nick, I believe we could manage something like this. He's the lieutenant who keeps everything running. I'm just sort of a figurehead. Nay," she laughed, "a mascot." As Cherise led us on a quick tour of the restaurant, Iris continued to sing my praises in a way that was cloying and embarrassing and made me feel like I was touring a college campus with my mother. I blushed, but Cherise smiled at me like she believed every word.

"Is your repairman from the company or an independent contractor?" I asked Cherise as we approached the center of the restaurant.

"Oh, these motors aren't so complicated. I give them a knock myself when I need to."

She flipped up a grate, revealing stairs like those that led down to New York City basements. "Well," Iris said, "I'm useless at this kind of thing. Why don't you go get a look, and I'll see about our hotel room."

"Hotel room?"

"Look outside. It's getting late."

A swatch of pink sky was visible in the doorway to the dining area, through which Iris disappeared before I could protest. Cherise offered a knowing smirk, but did me the kindness of letting it go quickly. At the bottom of the steps there was room to stand without crouching, and we simply walked back to the motor and stood next to it.

"The first thing to know is that all rotating restaurants are basically the same. Some different details, but it's like in geometry with circles and equilateral triangles. What's the word?"

"Similar."

"Every restaurant is similar. Different size, same technology."

She couldn't stop it while anyone was dining, but she opened different compartments and explained in great technical detail how it worked and what could go wrong. I surmised that the old bearings at Apogee were binding and forcing too much torque from the motor. She agreed. They had a spare set of bearings, she said, that "my lady" could buy. How strange it was, Cherise in her elegant dress and her stylish makeup and me in my Sunday second-best, down there in that industrial compartment, a refined dining room only six feet above us. It felt like a scene from a movie.

"I'm not above poaching a resourceful employee," she said as I followed her back into the dining area. "I can't create an assistant manager position, obviously. But start as a waiter, show your stuff, you'll move up quickly. You know the biz: lots of turnover—come on, you've got to prefer San Francisco to Fresno." Her glance around indicated that I should do the same. The sun had set while we were underneath the restaurant, and the city had been illuminated. Straight in front of me, the towers and scalloped cables of the Bay Bridge looked strung with Christmas lights. Far to my left, the same was true of the Golden Gate. The Transamerica Pyramid and the other skyscrapers around us were all lit, no blighted buildings blocking the view. It was beautiful.

"I've got family in Fresno," I said.

"Everyone has family in Fresno. Clackamas is my Fresno."

I didn't say anything.

"Sorry," she said. "It's not a take-it-or-leave-it offer. Leave it for now, call me when you want to take it."

"Do you have a card?"

Of course she did.

Iris was at the bar with an old fashioned. I asked if she was feeling poetic yet. She said she was always feeling poetic. After she wrote a check for the rotator bearings and arranged with the concierge to have them delivered to her car, if they would fit, she asked the bartender for a refill and led me out of the place with her full glass in her hand.

We didn't talk as she led me to our room, but I could see what she was saying with her body. She leaned her back against the glass of the elevator, resting her ass on the handrail. She sipped from her drink and watched me so directly I had to look away. In our hallway up on the twelfth floor, there was a swing in her hips that wasn't usually there. She was trying to make me imagine, I thought, ripping that dress off her and throwing her on the bed. I was imagining it. I felt I was being forced to imagine it.

The room, I was surprised to find, had two twin beds. She walked ahead of me and sat on the far one, the open-curtained window glittering behind her. "I wanted you to have a choice," she said. "Didn't want to feel I was forcing your hand." The confident stare she'd used in the elevator was wavering now. I walked forward until I stood between the two beds. In trying to think, I blocked myself from thinking.

She should have forced my hand, I thought. Give me a space to retreat into, and I will retreat. Offer me an empty bed and I'll sit on it. That's exactly what I did. For a moment she lost control of her face. When she regained it, she waited, clenching her lips, before she spoke. "I'm going to have a rinse off, then." She headed toward the bathroom with no swagger in her hips now, no request to be unzipped. I stayed on the edge of the bed, thinking about how either choice would have led to a lifetime of regret. They would be different regrets. Choosing her bed would have been the more interesting regret, and the lesser regret in general. It would not have added mass to the accumulating regrets about my inability to act. It could have had its own special drawer. Iris would have been the mathematical choice, and the artful one as well. But it was no longer a choice. The moment had passed, and now it was a fact.

I thought I heard her crying in the shower. As I listened, I realized she was making love to herself. It was an even sadder sound, not trying to be silent, not trying to be heard—just a series of small moans as regular as an old brake pad squeaking against its drum. The shower ran for a while even after they stopped, accompanied by the modulations of regular washing. Good thing hot water wasn't charged to the room. I lay down on the bed, facing the pretty window.

Iris came out wrapped in two towels, one around her body and one around her hair. She lay on the other bed, looking across at me. The small hotel towel showed me more of her legs than I'd seen before, creating the moment that made me realize appeal and availability formed an equation much too complex to be measured by a revelation of skin. The invitation was gone from her eyes.

"If she offers you a job, you should take it. You're not married to Fresno."

"I'm not sure what I want."

"Could be that you never will."

We fell asleep like that, facing each other across four feet of empty space. I know because she fell asleep first, still in her towels. I stayed up thinking of what Cherise had said about all revolving restaurants being geometrically similar. They were close enough to the same thing that the only important difference was what they looked out on. Our languishing restaurant had once sat atop the skyline of Waikiki with a line of patrons snaking out the door. Suppose you could pick up the whole thing, with Iris and me in it, and put it down on any tower in any city. Put us in a different place, would it be enough to give us different lives? That's where I drifted off, and fittingly, because such hypotheticals are already halfway to being dreams.

Sleep let go of her first as well, because when I woke in the morning she was back in her same dress. The magic trick, repeated, had no effect. The second morning it seemed tawdry, and I felt tawdry for witnessing it. It didn't help that her hair was a wreck from sleeping with it wrapped, a mess of weird curves that seemed the product of distorted gravity. But then, looking down at the clothes I had slept in, I was only one day behind her. All we had to put on were our shoes. We had no bags to pack. We didn't even need to see the front desk. We just left our key in the room and rode the elevator down to the garage. In her car big enough for two, we headed south again.

COYOTE

BATTLE CREEK COLLEGE

The premature clang of the morning bell had the young men half awake even before Eli and his crew burst into the bunkroom shouting that a cow had been murdered. Someone had led Columbia out of the barn during the night and slit her throat next to the well. Outside, it was the transparent black of empty and frozen air, not even the peaks of the Sierras yet lit to the west or a line of purple on the flat eastern horizon. The thermometers had the temperature at twenty-one. If they worked quickly, Eli said, she wouldn't have to go to waste. The young men were already out of their bunks. Letting an animal spoil was something nobody wanted, especially with Columbia, who of the fifty head they kept was the most noble-featured, the most loved.

When they got the floodlights on and made it out to the well, she was a dark lump on the ground. They saw that a thirteen-foot stream of blood had frozen over where it ran from her neck into a wide low puddle. She'd taken several steps before collapsing, and her forelegs looked like they'd been dipped in chocolate.

With a chain come-along they were able to pull her into the front loader of the backhoe without scooping up a mess of dirt, but its cab was too high to get them more than a few feet inside the barn door, and they had to fashion a sled on the top frame of the tractor's disc attachment. Eli commanded the whole thing, so that while five of the young men were getting Columbia into the front loader, five were wheeling the disc into position, five were gathering lead ropes from the tack room and tying them onto the disc, and the other thirteen were set to haul tables from the workshop into the barn, cover them with plastic sheeting, sterilize them, and prepare for the other requirements of butchery. The disc sank and cut grooves in the clay as fifteen of them strained to pull it, but there was no question of using the horses, which smelled Columbia's blood and were stamping and whinnying. The biggest challenge was lifting her carcass onto the table. A half-ton heifer divided among thirty people was fewer than fifty pounds each, but it was impossible for even half of them to get a clean purchase, so they looped furniture straps, tie downs, ropes, halters, and anything else at hand to allow those in the outer circle to shoulder a few pounds of the load. In one great heave, they got her up and onto the flat surface.

They worked in quiet concert. Eli said a few names, and those he called joined him in the tasks of skinning and gutting Columbia, of separating her into primal cuts, but none of the others went back to bed or to breakfast or milled about watching. Those not called to help Eli threw blankets over the horses and cows, since the barn door had been left open to bring down the temperature. When they ran out of horse blankets they brought blankets from their own beds. They broke up ice and transferred it to coolers to carry the meat, what would fit of it, to the deep freeze. Others set about washing and soaking the hide once Eli and his helpers had finished cutting it off. The work was serious and perhaps sad, but it was why most of them had come, for the power of a community in accord, doing the work that needed to be done, doing work that was apparent and abundant. There was a rhythm to it, a muscle memory, and none of the dwelling on past or future that came with idle time.

Only when the butchery was done, along with all the associated cleaning, did the eeriness of the situation start to settle in. They'd sprung into action together, and done it well, and had left out of their minds that what started the process was the murder of a favored cow. A killing that served no purpose, that seemed too far afield even for random malice. Especially after what had happened to the dog. They all sat together around the well, still warm from their labor. Sunlight put a shine on the snowcaps to the west now, and a damp peach light was in the air. The diorama of cow's blood was still frozen in the dirt, but the top was starting to shimmer and bead with droplets.

Who could have done such a thing? The first hypothesis was bored townie punks. Home-cooked meth had come to nearby Bishop recently, if in a small way, and unpredictable behavior had stopped being unfamiliar. But several of the students pointed out that it was a bit hard to imagine someone getting freaked out on meth, driving thirty miles on country roads in the dark, finding a cow—and not just any cow—in the barn, getting her out to center of campus, and slicing her throat, not to mention doing so without making enough noise to wake anyone up.

The quiet that followed was uncomfortable.

"Anybody got a crazy ex?" Neil asked with a stillborn chuckle.

It was Wesley Denniston who spoke up, a wiry second-year with the haircut of an orphan, which always made a surprise out of the clarity, the beauty, of his voice, even though he was never shy about using it. In every seminar, his voice was the first raised, and it was absent the upward lilt of a question mark. Everyone's eyes went to him. Eli stared him into the dust, but Eli was behind the rest of the group where they couldn't see him, and Wesley went on anyway.

"We all do," he said. "Hugo."

"That seems a pretty wild speculation," Eli said.

"Just how wild?" Wesley said, staring right back.

WESLEY

I know Paul tells us our salvation is not by works but by faith. When James argues for the importance of works, however, he is not contradicting Paul. He says that a faith apart from works is dead, that a living faith will produce works. The point is that acts are not irrelevant. What draws most of us, and certainly me, to Battle Creek College is the idea not just that faith affects works, but that works affect faith. So when we are lugging sandbags or harvesting vegetables by hand or working all together to drive cattle through the corral to tag, horn, brand, and vaccinate them, that is its own kind of prayer. By adding it to traditional prayer, we enrich our faith. Many know the motto Simple Work, Complex Faith, but few understand it. Still, the school works well as a magnet: the ones who seek it are the ones who belong. Those who don't believe in work don't come.

Hugo was the exception. From the moment he arrived I sensed something off about him. He lacked a certain gravity. He was not serious enough. During work hours, students' faces displayed the turning over and sorting out of the day's lectures; you could see the smelting of ore into iron through the furnace of labor. But not with Hugo. He would look off at the mountains, or get lost in the sunset, and his pace would slow. If it was line work, he would throw off the rhythm of the whole crew. And his quiet in the seminar was unlike those who waited, listened, and processed thoughtfully before speaking, like Eli. Hugo's silence was simply disengaged from the high life of the mind this place is designed to serve.

Eli, on the other hand, looked like a healthy thirty-year-old man even though he was only twenty-two. He was the type who had looked full-grown at thirteen. He looked like a cowboy, like a man who knew the land through a communion with the One who made it. He had finished his degree two years earlier and was in the second year of his ranch steward fellowship. He guided us not just in the upkeep of our crops and livestock, but in the classroom, where he was a sort of graduate assistant, and he let the students air their first thoughts and prejudices before diving in with a comment, or more often a question, that made clear the issue, or would rattle around in thirty skulls during our duty hours. Both the professors and Pastor Dale shifted their tone when talking to Eli, conversing with him as with an equal.

You can see why I could not have predicted or even believed that Hugo's bad spirit could worm its way into this man. And yet the Book tells us that Adam and Eve fell, that the great David fell, that Saul fell, that even the Apostles denied and doubted their Lord. So it was some speck in my own eye, a naiveté or a boyish lack of confidence, that kept me from seeing the corruption of Eli sooner. How I wish that I had seen it sooner. But once I saw it I could not simply let it go. A living faith sometimes requires action.

ELI

I'd worried about Hugo from the start. Most kids came to the college with a drawer of secret anger, which the ranch work helped them burn off safely. You could see their fathers perched on their shoulders, doubting them. Others came with good-boy haircuts and a missionary good cheer. Hugo had a look I hadn't seen before here. He was soft in the middle and had a mooning look in his eyes that the other students didn't care for. I assigned him to my own work detail so I could look out for him and make sure he adjusted okay. Our main duty that fall was irrigation, and we'd ride out along the canals kicking the taps on and off, checking levels, and mucking out any debris we happened to find. September in Battle Creek meant sweltering afternoons with cold evenings, and as the sun got low one of those first days, Hugo, who was still an unsure rider, had to dismount to put on his coat. I rode up next to him and said:

"Don't you know how to grip a horse with your legs?"

"Can't say that I do."

"There's no getting around learning."

"People say I'm a slow learner. If that's true, I never minded it."

He seemed to realize that he was being standoffish, and that my attempt at ribbing him was simply my trying to be sensitive without giving the impression that he needed sensitivity. We were out by a field of leeks, and their green stalks were reaching up out of the soil like a thousand lizard paws, and looking out over them, he said, "They're happy to have company tonight." I didn't know yet that this was one of his mannerisms, making these odd qualitative statements. Columbia was the most beautiful cow, he said, which agreed with the consensus, and Galahad was the most beautiful horse, which diverged from it. One day he pointed up at the Sierras, at a peak just separate from three others linked in a ridge, and told me it was the saddest mountain. I didn't know if his strange pronouncements were sincere or an affectation, and I didn't really want to know. I came to love them. But the first time I heard one, I didn't know how to respond. I just told him what I knew: we'd be pulling up those leeks soon, and planting turnips.

WESLEY

I saw Hugo pulling up handfuls of early carrots on an afternoon at the end of September, when the ground was still tender and clumpy from the late summer rains and clung in dark walnuts to the pale orange icicles. He stacked them in the basket of his t-shirt, which distended into a lumpy mass. As he shuffled from the garden to the barn like that, a few carrots would sluice out the side of his bundle, and he'd have to stoop down and grope with his hand to retrieve them.

In the barn he walked back and forth between Columbia and Galahad, feeding them each a carrot at a time and rubbing their ears, their faces, so intent, almost in a trance, that he took no notice of me standing in the doorway until I confronted him about what he was doing.

"It's from the vegetable garden," he said, "not the crops."

"So rather than stealing money from the college, you're stealing food from its students."

"I could never appreciate this carrot," he said, holding one aloft next to Galahad, "the way she appreciates it." He smiled at me. The Bible makes no distinction between a smiling sinner and a sneaking one, but I felt then and I still feel after searching and prayer the conviction that it is a meaningful one.

"You don't understand—"

"That's not a very Christian welcome." Eli spoke from the doorway, where I'd been standing before I'd advanced on Hugo. Eli nodded me out of the barn, and as I went he clapped me on the shoulder and said, "Don't worry. It won't happen again." Remember that at the time I had not learned to distrust him.

The next day Columbia's milk turned pink, and we called the vet, thinking she had an infection. The vet smelled the milk, and then tasted it, surprising all of us there in the barn who thought it harbored deadly bacteria. He said he'd seen it before, mostly with gentle old timers and farm dowagers. The color was from the carotene and was perfectly harmless. If we stopped feeding her carrots, he said, it would return to normal in a few days. But the milk never went back to white.

ELI

Irrigation amounts to making sure the right dirt is wet, and thus it's muddy work. But it was even muddier than usual the day in October when we found a dog struggling to swim in the canal out by the nut trees. I kid you not, it was a corgi, scratching with its stub legs at the bank but unable to claw its way out and about dead with exhaustion. I leapt in with my boots on and grabbed the poor thing, which was like a soaked and wriggling roll of carpet, and leaned against the wall of the ditch to hand it off to Hugo and Claude. We rode back to the main campus with me coated in mud all down my front side and with my boots, which had about turned into pitchers of slop, in my saddlebags. Hugo led his horse with one hand and the surprisingly obedient corgi with the other, by a lead rope he'd tied around her belly. Claude jabbered the whole way back about how corgis were supposed to be a smart breed so he didn't know why one would jump into an irrigation ditch with the body type of a hot dog.

The outdoor shower on the back side of the house was like the stall in a cheap bathroom, with just walls on either side but no door. I'd been in the hot water a long time, getting my fingernails clean, degunking the creases between my toes, the cracks of my thighs, mud just about everywhere it can go, before I looked over my shoulder and saw Hugo standing where he had a line of sight. This was far from the first time I'd caught one of the guys here watching me, but it was the first time the culprit had the nerve to keep watching, to smile openly, after being discovered, rather than tucking his head and hurrying off. So what the hell, I thought. I closed my eyes, tilted my head back, and ran my hands through my hair as I turned around to give him the full show.

WESLEY

You can tell a thing by its absence. The first absence I noticed was Hugo's during breaks and study hours and our nightly stretches of free time. It was common enough for Eli to be off during these stretches, pounding stakes or killing snakes or fixing up the truck. All the details that didn't fall within student work routines were his domain. Because Columbia's milk remained pink, I knew I should be able to catch Hugo pilfering from the garden or in the barn, and yet I could never find him at either. Then I noticed I could never find him at all during those hours. Then I noticed that when I tried to find Eli to express my concern, I could never find Eli either. But the idea did not occur to me then. It remained too impossible for even the imagination.

It was with genuine curiosity, genuine worry, that I too disappeared from our unscheduled hours, searching every corner and level of the barn, searching in and under the pickup, and riding horseback down the alleys between fields and along the perimeter of campus, searching for my missing compatriots, to no avail. I'll admit that I began to despair, as if it were an important page missing from a book of philosophy I was reading, a page offering definitions that would be referenced again later.

A broken sprinkler head shifted me from one despair to another. I found it flooding the corner of the farmhouse green on one of those dusk rides, and I hopped off and waded into the mud to screw a cap onto it. I went out to clean off at the mud shower, which no one used at that time because it was too cold and work hours were long over, but as I rounded the corner to the back side of the dormitory, I spotted a pair of boots under the wall of the cubby, the feet in them shifting gently from side to side. As I crept around to see in the faint purple light, the scene revealed itself: they were both clothed, but Eli had Hugo lifted and pressed against the back wall of the shower, and Hugo's legs were wrapped around Eli's waist, crossed at the ankles, and the two of them were kissing.

"The Devil has brought you together, but I will pry you apart," I shouted, but it came out as a whisper. The Devil had quieted my voice, I thought, and I confess that I fled. When I came back again on several other evenings, I also found my voice missing and my conviction sapped. I could not even speak on the one when I found them both nude, and Hugo kneeling in front of Eli, working Eli's lap with his mouth. The greater their indiscretions, the more my power was blocked, such that I found myself paralyzed by the spectacle and unable to look away. Eli's eyes were closed so he could not see my face, but I could see his, and it was caught in a fire of what at the time I called ecstasy. But the roots of the word ecstasy are the Greek *ek*, for "out of," and *stasis*, for "the place where one stands," though it was not that he was outside of himself. No, the right word was the one that means to be held by, to be occupied. The look on his face was that of a man possessed.

ELI

How many months does it take to fall in love?

The question is phrased wrong.

It doesn't happen like the flipping of a switch, like the addition of a current to a dormant wire. Falling in love is like being flooded with water so that you feel it running down your head and body even as it rises around your ankles and immerses you.

Hugo named the damn dog Mavis and taught her to live in the southwest corner of the barn near the door, next to Columbia. The cattle didn't have stalls like the horses did; they could wander into any place they liked, but after Hugo had guided Columbia enough times to her place near the door, through which the snowcapped mountains could be seen sleeping on top of the orchard, she had adopted it as her own.

The students did not like the idea of adopting a pet and grumbled indistinctly about it, but really making that kind of call was something about which they knew to defer to me. I fended them off by arguing she was a herding breed, though she did not herd and seemed only to care for food and petting. In truth, the dog would have gone to a shelter, kill- or non-, on the day she showed up if anyone but Hugo had taken her in. That was one of the things that drew me to him—his renunciation of the utilitarian view of the land we all took, and the way he looked at a dog or a cow or a horse and wanted it to be nothing more than what it was. When we weren't sneaking off, he spent most of his free time in the barn, rubbing Mavis's belly, talking to Columbia, and currying and otherwise tending to Galahad. The way he acted not just with these animals but with an onion, a lizard, made me believe that I myself should love them all better too.

WESLEY

As I have said, the gravity of their sins somehow prevented me from acting. A much smaller sin, a simpler one, is what freed me. Early one morning I walked by the barn and saw Eli inside, offering a carrot to Columbia all by himself. That was it. Let it not be said that I took rash or hasty action. I sought first the counsel of Pastor Dale. I waited for him to ride out on Lancelot one Tuesday after our theology class, and I rode out after him on Gawain, neglecting my work duties to do so, though for the purpose of speaking to the pastor, allowances were made.

"You're in a great trial," he said before I could even begin. I looked away. "It's all over your face, kid. Lay it on me."

"I fear for Eli's soul."

"You've got a real atavistic diction, you know that?"

"I'd call it nostalgic."

"Potato, po-tah-to."

He kept his boots clean, kept his jeans clean, despite not being shy with the dirt. It was a simple trick, but quite comforting, as was his cowboy-gospel mien, which, casual though it was, was rooted in a deep and abiding faith. I tried not to sound nostalgic and instead sounded only like a child.

"He's up to something bad."

Pastor Dale held up his palm to try to stop me.

"Something very bad. And I've known for weeks, and I've tried to stop it."

He raised his hand two inches, and I stopped.

"Who is his spiritual leader?" he said. "Has Eli been named one of *your* sheep? Who hears his confession weekly? Your concern is good hearted, but look first to the beam in your own eye."

"But he's failed to confess this, or you wouldn't take it so lightly."

"If his confessions are partial that's a matter for me. Mostly for him, really. A little for me. Trust in me. Trust in the Lord. He expects his sheep to return to him. He does not expect them never to stray, for who knows their nature better than Him?"

He waited to see if I had further objections. He clearly did not welcome them.

"Cheer up, kid," he said, spurring Lancelot, and I had no choice but to either chase after him or let him go.

With effort I could mind his counsels during the day. But for a week I had trouble sleeping. With my eyes closed, the theater of my mind flashed only to the scene of Hugo's buttocks saddled on his heels, of his head doing that thing to Eli, of Eli's long body arching backwards and his face the face of his possession. And then in the darkness of the bunkroom I would lose track of whether my eyes were closed at all. After a week of this torment, which I suspected was the prompting of God to do what must be done, I took my knife from my footlocker, unfolded it silently, and padded silently across the room to Hugo's bed. I scraped the knife twice against the skin of his neck as if shaving him, just enough to leave an abrasion and see if he would wake. When his eyelids fluttered open, I pressed the flat of the blade into his lips, and I whispered to him, perhaps I hissed, "Agents of the Devil cannot abide in holy places. You must cast yourself out or be cast out. Your Master is nothing compared to ours. Your faith is small compared to ours, and ours will not flinch. You must leave tomorrow. You are exiled from the lands of the Lord."

His eyes were wide with awe and terror. They seemed to glow in the dark. Knowing that I would be unable to sleep after this encounter, I walked out into the frigid night air, but my body felt no cold.

ELI

I've never been a light sleeper, so I chalk it up to providence that I woke that night. A rustling sound repeated across the bunkroom that was not quite the wind, not quite a squirrel on the roof. My eyes adjusted, and I thought I saw Hugo standing up next to his bed, but as I strained to see in his posture hints of what was troubling him, it became clear that the height and the build and the carriage were not his. I crept closer and saw that the exposed flat buttocks, matte gray in the scant light, were certainly not his. The pauper's haircut, the military stance—Wesley Denniston.

As soon as I got an angle enough to see Wesley stroking his erection and prodding Hugo's sleeping lips with it, my concern for stealth disappeared, and I wrapped my fists in his shirt and lifted him off the floor, hearing the fabric at his armpits rip. He went rigid, locking his wide white eyes on mine as I shouldered open the door and carried him out into the yard and threw him in a horse trough. His limbs came unlocked when he landed in the frigid water, churning a storm out of it. I thought of helping him get out, but decided against it.

Back inside, once my eyes had adjusted back out of the starlight, I saw that a few of the students were sitting up and looking at me quizzically, sleepily. "Coyote," I said. They nodded and lay back down. After crawling back into my bed I couldn't sleep, keeping sentinel watch over Hugo, prepared for Wesley to return with more drastic intentions. He didn't return at all, though, and I was kept up the rest of the night by the worry that I'd killed him. It was October now. The lows were in the 40s.

I went out in the morning to look for him, while the other students were just rising. He was fast asleep in the barn. He'd hung out his wet clothes, curled up with Columbia, and covered himself with hay. He showed up at breakfast as if nothing had happened.

WESLEY

Hugo did not heed my warning. He and Eli shifted their trysts to some other nook I was unable to discover, but their sly public glances and sensitive friendship went on undeterred. This time I did not hesitate. After allowing two days for him to leave our midst, I snuck away from my planting detail and packed his bags in the bunkroom. I grabbed the pickup keys from the office, threw his bags in the cab, and watched him all day until he ambled back alone through the already bare stone fruit trees. Just as he was turning to head out of the treeline, I roped him by the ankle, and he fell flat on his face. By the time he rolled over I had a sock stuffed in his mouth and a handkerchief between his teeth to tie it in place. Kneeling on his shoulders, I socked him twice to stop him struggling, and when he went gentle I tied his wrists together between his legs and back out around his waist. Then I tied his ankles together and looped it to the other rope. Hoisting him onto the tailgate, I looped his tethers with bungee cords to the hooks in the bed of the truck.

"If you jump out you'll get dragged to death," I told him. "You stay calm, and I'll keep the ride gentle."

Nonetheless he kept hooking his feet on the bed the whole way, trying to jimmy his hips onto the edge, and I kept having to take hard turns to shake him back into the box. The roads out there all looked like they led to nowhere. I didn't mind him thinking maybe he was on his way to get buried. Forcing him out would obviously take more fear than I'd delivered thus far. I didn't want him to think me incapable of it, and at the same time I struggled not to believe myself capable of it.

No one was about in Ridgecrest. It was the dominion of dust. A bus that would stop here despite the dearth of passengers seemed an idea from the realm of myth or fable, and I bought his ticket half believing that the driver would lose heart and retire before he ever made it to the station. Nonetheless, I spent the time before its scheduled arrival in the bed of the truck with Hugo, explaining to him the stakes of the situation.

"I know the Devil will draw you back to Eli like a magnet," I said, "so I will be the other pole of the magnet, repulsing you. I will kill a thing you love each time you return."

His eyes were defiant, but when the miracle bus arrived, I cut the ropes and slipped the ticket to Denver by way of Barstow into his pocket. I left the knife open and loose in my palm, and he got on the bus without complaint. He watched me the whole time with the Devil's eyes, but I watched him right back with the eyes of the Holy Spirit and I saw, I thought I saw, the spirit in him quell.

ELI

I loved perhaps nothing more about Hugo than his tenderness to animals, but I also wanted to teach him the danger of loving things this way, of loving animals raised for stock or bred for labor. I taught that lesson only to myself. Hugo disappeared from campus. The police weren't interested. He was young. He'd taken his things. They took my suspicions of Wesley to be a silly grudge.

I took Mavis out all over the compound hoping she'd lead me to Hugo, but I didn't know whether she found nothing because there was nothing to find or because she was as bad at tracking as she was at everything else. For five days I searched, and I had to consider that falling out of love also had no requisite number of months, that it could go extinct in a moment, that the faucet could simply turn off.

On the fifth night Mavis smelled something out by the nut orchard, near where we'd first found her. She tapped at the top of the irrigation canal with one paw but would not go in the water. After commanding her to sit and wait, I hopped across and walked into what looked in the twilight like a palace of dark colonnades. I scanned the orchard floor for disturbed earth. Then I heard a very poor imitation of a horse's nicker, and when I looked up there he was.

We made love in the dirt. We said little. We'd said it.

Lying there on our backs, I saw him fighting great emotion.

"I couldn't help it," he said. "I won't come back again."

"Let's get you back to your bunk."

"You don't understand."

He was up, pulling his jeans over his naked hips. He tossed his boxer briefs into my lap.

"Don't forget me," he said, trotting away toward the road holding his shirt in his fist.

The next day, Mavis disappeared, and I figured she'd followed him off, that maybe he was camping or living somewhere nearby, but I didn't have anything to track the dog that was tracking him. The week after that, Claude found her floating in the irrigation ditch near where we'd first saved her and where I'd met with Hugo, and I figured she had smelled him on the other side again, and without me there to stop her, had lost patience and tried to get across. Claude and I buried her there in the lane between orchard and field. Then I sent him back, and I ran through the orchard. I searched it by day and by night, by dusk and dawn, but there was no trace of him.

He found me again a month later, with that unmistakable hamfisted nicker issuing from a field of sloping grazeland, and I tramped the grass until I spotted him sitting cross-legged in it, invisible except to me. We flattened a patch of fresh alfalfa that left long red stripes along his back and my thighs. Again I could tell that his instinct was to run off. I'd seen deer and elk before, spooked, their bodies tensed for flight. But he stayed a few minutes because he sensed my need.

"I won't come back again." He rolled against me and put his head on my shoulder and rubbed his hand on my belly and said, "This is the most beautiful man."

I almost asked him then what had brought him here. He was nothing like the rest, whose seeking followed only paved roads. He was so secret. Why had he come to a place for which he knew he was too gentle? But I restrained myself from asking what had brought him so as not to ruin my little dream that the answer he would give me was God.

BATTLE CREEK COLLEGE

All day the ranch had smelled of coal and beef fat. The odor kept in everyone's mind the sight of great pearly globs of the fat, sheets of it, peeled away and tossed in a trash barrel, there being too much other work to worry about making tallow. They ground the chucks and mixed a vat of meatloaves and Saran-wrapped rectangular portions that stacked neatly in the freezer, displacing loaves of bread that were buttered and grilled to round out the meals. The short ribs, shanks, rounds, and briskets were first on a low fire in the morning so they'd melt in time for dinner. The ribs and a long loin roast were cooked for lunch, but the meal was a somber affair, the ribs eaten slowly, reluctantly. Despite the talk of honoring Columbia by making our best use of her, no one was quite ready to chew on her bones.

By dinner that melancholy had given way to celebration not of the spirit and sacrifice of the stock animal but rather to the conviviality that comes with rich and abundant food, that comes with unctuous chins and hands and the jeans they're wiped on. An early sunset gave way to a shroud of night around the same floodlights they'd labored under in the morning. The pool of blood had thawed and soaked into the ground, leaving a dark and fertile streak of soil. There was no beer with the feast, but there was singing. No hymns tonight, just songs from high school dances, songs from the radio, songs from the radio of years past, all carrying out who knows how far toward the mountains.

No one asked where Wesley was, but he could hear their song out on the perimeter, where he'd stopped Gawain and turned off his flashlight to offer his ear to the night, sorting the crickets from the frogs and the scattered howling of coyotes and the muffled drumming of drunks shooting target practice on the outskirts of Bishop. The crunch of a man's boots in the dirt was a different order of noise, its own category, and not hard to tell from the others. But tonight there was nothing. Every sound was organic except, when he set Gawain to walking again, the step of a shod horse. It was a waste of time, anyway. Hugo left long trails of boot prints every time he came, traveling the quarry road that ran a few miles north of campus. If Hugo had come again, it would be clear enough by daylight. Wesley supposed it was time to think about, then, what other reasons had drawn him out here.

No one asked where Eli was, either. They'd gotten used to his truancy, his distance. The first-years barely knew it was different. He was in the barn, standing outside the bolted door of Galahad's stall. Without exactly meaning to he'd taken note of a pointed shovel within arm's reach and a hay fork only yards away. If you paid close attention, it only took two to show a pattern. But he had neither tool in his hand. He had oats, and Galahad's expressive lips were scooping them up, rubbing his palm with the soft rubber of their skin. As long as Eli had food, Galahad let Eli pet him over the ears, above his bulbous eye, and down his long forehead to his muzzle. "How right he was about you," Eli said to him. Even the nostrils of horses had fine muscles. Every fine little hair had its own luster. He reached down to the bucket for another handful of oats, wondering when he would ever sleep again.

DENTISTS

From my window, I counted the shadows in the Maliks' driveway. I could only see them when they passed in front of the open garage door, backlit by the opener's dim bulb, but it was easy to make out Dr. Malik's silhouette. Like many tall doctors, he was gently hunched from leaning close to his patients, and he was a little soft in the back and the belly. Mrs. Malik was not hard to distinguish either. She was taller than both her girls, and though at various times one of the three of them would disappear back inside, she mostly stood behind them with a hand on the shoulder of each, as if they were taking a shadow portrait. In the daylight their hijabs and their family resemblance made them easy to confuse with one another at a quick glance, but these circumstances changed them. In the darkness, Mrs. Malik's headscarf looked like a trendy bob, whereas the lack of light played a different trick with the girls, somehow turning the smooth fabric of their coverings choppy and angular. It was their posture that distinguished the two girls now. Amina, who was in high school, stood upright and patient like her mother. Safiya, on the other hand, leaned and pulled and made movements toward the house or the vehicle.

The back of their Acura minivan was open, and Dr. Malik made trips in and out of the house to load it. It was October, and my window was cracked open. Their whispers made a hissing sound in the night that I'd first mistaken for a faucet left on in the bathroom. I was curious about what they were saying, but I didn't want to make a sound by opening the window further. I didn't want to alarm them.

I had some idea why they were leaving under the cover of night. I'd heard about the executive order during my restaurant shift after school. After the Baitul Hameed Mosque bombing, and the ones of the previous week, not to mention the assorted beatings and killings around the country, the government had said they lacked the resources to shield Muslims from violence, and were asking all practicing Muslims to relocate to designated Protection Villas—some cleared-out apartment blocks—where the National Guard could watch over them. As unappealing as that prospect was, when I heard some of my coworkers cheer the order, and others saying that the last thing Muslims deserved was protection, I could imagine worse things than National Guard protection.

My father had taken a harder tack. He'd been drinking in a kitchen chair when I got home, looking like a bad actor trying on a Eugene O'Neill character. He was playing at a roughness belied by his slender, slouched shoulders, his faded olive button-down, his softly shaven cheeks, his thin-framed glasses. He looked the very picture of The Liberal in Defeat. Had he auditioned for such a role, he'd have been dismissed as too on the nose.

He and I had been close before the last year. Our distaste for one another had not come about in the usual way of an arrogant teenager shoving off from authority. It was more personal, more like a marriage that had soured. He'd started telling me that as I got closer to adulthood, not seeing what was happening in front of me became a personal failing. I would shrug and suggest he was being hysterical. We were in an ugly swing of the political pendulum, but would swing back. After I'd rebuffed him like that a few times, his tone toward me changed. He began speaking about how good a heart I'd had as a child. How open I'd been to the world. How sensitive to other people's misfortunes. It was his elegy for me, which he delivered in front of me, as if I'd died young. What had happened?

he'd ask my mother, who was only a prop in the act for which I was the audience. Now, he said—this was his real mantra—I was "like the ones who had let it happen." My mother would retreat to her room. I'd roll my eyes and do the same, not without a parting shot about him acting like a frail old maid. I'd started thinking of him as having an illness. A weakness of character, and a degenerative one.

Sitting at the table with his bottle that night, he started telling me about shoes. Rooms had been filled with them. Mountains of old leather husks. Warehouses brimming with them. You wouldn't believe you could fill a space that big with shoes. And if you imagined a person in each pair? They don't teach those kind of details anymore, he said. He'd asked some of my history teachers. Jewelry, furs, clothing. Gold teeth. They'd had a whole staff of dentists.

I went upstairs. I actually did share a lot of my dad's ideas, and probably would have shared them more forcefully had I not associated them with him. He had been raised under a peaceful sign, I thought, and had never developed the fortitude necessary for dark times. But even if that fortitude was a quality I credited myself with, I did have trouble sleeping that night. That's why I was up to see my neighbors' hurried departure. They went down the street with their headlights off, and I watched, as I'm sure they did, to see if any bedroom lights would turn on as the van passed. None did. When the vehicle rounded the corner, it occurred to me that I would never see the Maliks again.

I knew so little about them. Dr. Malik had been four when his parents moved to the US from Pakistan. His wife had been a fetus when her family immigrated. Conceived in Lahore, born in Houston. The girls, of course, had lived their whole lives here. If not for my father, one of the only people on the street who spoke with them regularly, I don't suppose I would have known their names. They were fashionable people, he said. A bit bougie, even. I didn't see it, but what room did I have to argue? With regret for the blank spaces I'd left behind their cutouts, I stared at their garage door, which Dr. Malik had rolled down manually and left open about six inches, as you would for a cat. I didn't even know whether they had a cat. If they did, and if they had left it, the house was still a home to something. If not, the place was now purely archeological.

My house was dark as I crept down the stairs. The kitchen light was off, meaning my father was no longer there, but the oscillating fan outside his room was off as well, and he was unable to sleep without it. My mother was working her night shift at the hospital, and it wouldn't even be her lunch break yet. Streetlight through the kitchen window backlit the rangy arms of houseplants and fuzzed a pile of dishes and cups with gray. With our own house as seemingly abandoned as the one next door, I simply left through the front door.

The Maliks' garage door rolled up silently and easily. Dr. Malik's Lexus, resting inside, would be a boon for someone. Inside, I turned on the lights. I wasn't scared to do so, and realized how surreal it was that in the course of a day it had become safer for me to be in their house than for them to. The laundry room floor was tiled in large, symmetrical diamonds that continued into the kitchen. No sign of a litter box. The lid of the washing machine was open as if waiting for a load. The kitchen was clean and well appointed. There wasn't much in the way of Islamic decor. A few nicely framed bits of a foreign script, Urdu I presumed, hung on the walls. The turquoise backsplash had a vaguely South Asian flair to it, but overall I felt more like I'd walked into a cover of *House Beautiful* than a home of the devout. There was something on the island, though, set out in front of the bar stools. It was black velvet embroidered with golden thread and little circular mirrors, and it stood up on the counter like a hat. Thinking it *was* a hat, I picked it up and found a teapot underneath. I crouched down to look at it more closely. I don't know that I'd seen a more beautiful artifact. The gleaming brass was laid over with a thick stripe of royal blue, with a careful, complex fretwork of the brass below tracing the outlines of branches, leaves, and flowers. It was as if all of the intricate and detailed Pakistani designs I'd expected to find suffusing the house had been concentrated into the teapot, hidden there under its cozy.

The refrigerator contained so many vegetables that they didn't all fit in the crisper. Zucchini sat in a plastic bag on the shelf. I picked up a half a bunch of celery, which had gone limp. Two-percent milk. Commercial Greek yogurt. A rotisserie chicken. Margherita pizzas in the freezer. Pistachio ice cream. I don't know what I'd been expecting. Muslims did not eat pork; the women wore scarves or veils; they prayed in the morning and evening, maybe more, on mats that they faced toward Mecca. And with that I'd exhausted my knowledge of the religion, though for some reason I'd always felt I had a deep, or deep enough, understanding of it.

Peeking into a nook off the dining room, I thought I might see mats laid out on the floor. The room was empty, making me think I was correct about this being their prayer room, but the only mats were hung from the wall like tapestries. On one little delicately engraved table was a group of beaded strings, something like rosaries, but in varied colors. I would have thought they would take those with them, needing them wherever they went. I would understand more soon enough. I didn't bother with the computer in the office, figuring it would be password protected and not wanting to sit down, to allow time to slip by unnoticed. The entryway had a nicely constructed set of cubbies, mostly filled with shoes. They all had a taste for chic footwear, and while surely they had each departed with a pair on their feet, it must have been hard to leave so many behind. It was no warehouse, but now there was no looking at the sets of shoes without seeing their empty spaces as their defining features.

I should take off my own shoes, I thought, but it seemed too late for that.

In horror films, heading up the stairs can be a fatal mistake. There was a bit of that chill as I took to the steps, though the danger I felt was not a physical one. I felt as if I was about to walk in on the Malik family's murdered bodies, though I knew I'd seen them drive away not an hour ago. The hallway was quiet and still. Even with the light on, it had a particular emptiness.

But the girls' rooms were girls' rooms. The one with clothes on the floor, boy-band posters over an unmade bed, and rumpled lined paper and worksheets spread chaotically around the desk belonged, I assumed, to Safiya, the younger daughter. That would leave as Amina's room a spotless, well-decorated space, appointed in an adult style. The walls were painted a latte color. An oval mirror in an ornate silvered frame hung above a writing desk. A small jewelry tree sat on the dresser, adorned with a few dangling necklaces and earrings. The one exception to order was an overcrowded bookshelf, with paperbacks stacked sideways on top of the properly shelved books, filling in all the negative space. There was a stack on top of the shelf as well, with library labels on the bottoms of their spines.

The master bedroom was not in a normal state. It did not appear ransacked, but it didn't look untouched either. Piles of women's shirts were on the floor in front of a dresser. A pile of pants was on the bed, which appeared to be a California king. I had seen the rooms of messy people—my mother's side of my parents' room—and this was distinctly different. An empty duffel bag sat outside a slightly open closet door, looking deflated. Beyond the visual evidence of the Maliks' life in this room, there was a tour of scents that I believe could have led me through the space if I closed my eyes: sandalwood, soap, jasmine. I was sure the fragrances could be mapped to different parts of the bedroom, but I could not read that map, and so they seemed to me as jumbled as this hastily evacuated chamber.

I opened one of the small top drawers of the dresser: socks. I opened the next drawer. In the front was a pile of women's underwear, a bit drab, showing too many times through the wash. Behind that was an equal-sized pile of silkier, lacier stuff in a variety of colors. Behind that, but not exactly tucked away, was a sleek purple vibrator. I picked it up by its white plastic handle and held it aloft. Its surface was nearly reflective. I turned it on, and it waggled its long finger at me. I'd never held such a thing before and I didn't feel comfortable doing so. I turned it off and put it back.

On Mrs. Malik's nightstand was a book I recognized. My mother had tried to convince me to read it. On its cheesy cover, a mother was standing on the beach, holding her young daughter and looking out at the sea. Elena Ferrante, the cover read. They had left their smartphones in a cluster on the bed, which puzzled me until I thought of the GPS trackers they contained.

It was the bathroom, though, that was in the greatest state of disarray. Socks on the floor, other clothes. In the bathtub were three piles of women's hair, and though I had not seen their hair uncovered before, except for Safiya's when she was younger, I knew whom each pile belonged to as easily as if they had been labeled. What is it that makes hair younger? That distinguishes the hair of a woman from the hair of a girl? But I knew that the long, silky pile of black hair was Mrs. Malik's, and that the two thinner, duller, messier piles belonged to her daughters.

One of the dual sinks was furry with the salt-and-pepper trimmings of Dr. Malik's beard. The other sink was stained with a maroon hair dye, the open box on its side nearby, empty. In between the two was a just-opened cylinder of styling wax. I could tell it was new because the plastic safety seal was right next to it. Cosmetics were loosely scattered around the counter. All the lids were back on, but they had not been put back in the open case that held a deeper repository of shades and colors. Glinting amid the mess was a simple gold heart-shaped locket on a thin chain. I picked it up to look inside. There were two portraits, one of each girl.

I did not put it down. The redhats would be by in a day or two to go through the place, and I did not want to think of it melted or thrown in the trash, or the pictures replaced with those of two white girls. This was the last I wanted to see of the place. I knew I would not sleep again that night, that I would lie in bed with that feeling in my stomach, and it would not be until sometime in the midmorning that physiological need would wrestle down worry and I, like my mother, would sleep through the day.

I turned off each light as I retreated through the house by the same path I'd entered. I rolled up the garage door quietly and left it slightly open for the cat that did not exist. My house and the Maliks' house were dark twins in the night, the facades only superficially different. As I walked back inside, I thought of my mother for some reason, and how she was in a different world than I was at the moment, an interior world whose lights never went off, where staff still wandered the halls, sat at the stations, and tended patients, some of whom would be awake as well. I didn't think anything more about her. I just pictured her there.

As I crossed through the kitchen, the lights flipped on, and I froze where I stood. My father was in the same chair I'd seen him in earlier, watching me. His hand was still stretched out to the light switch next to him. I felt a momentary, reflexive disdain for him, and then a wave of shame for that reaction. He had always judged me. Maybe in the way all fathers judge their sons. Maybe worse. But oh how he was judging me now. From the first moment, his eyes were on the locket that dangled from my fist, as if he'd known where to look. He never met my eyes. I knew he was thinking of the shoes, the dentists. Living under his judgment so long had been like holding up a boot trying to crash down on me. To finally see myself through his eyes—to see what I was holding, to know where I'd been—was like letting it. How I'd judged him, too, and for so long. For his softness, for his aura of defeat. For his preemptive disappointment in me. But now I could see that he was so defeated because he had seen the future. He had seen the future long ago, and now it was here.

ACKNOWLEDGMENTS

There are many to whom this book owes its thanks. To my editor, Nicola Mason, for bringing the book into being and helping it become what it is. To my mentors, Liza Wieland and Steve Yarbrough, whose guidance from my earliest writing days has helped me be able to always see the way forward. To those who helped me hone and improve these stories: Erin Cook, Carole Firstman, Sally Vogl, Phyllis Brotherton, Jim Schmidt, and especially Elizabeth Schulte Martin. To friends smarter than I am, without whose knowledge and expertise many of these stories would not have been possible: Maryam Attia, Samina Najmi, Bob Allaire, Tim Ellison, Jesse Rorabaugh, and Jessica Sweet.

I am also thankful for the literary magazine editors who first published these stories: David Lynn and Caitlin Horrocks of *Kenyon Review*; Carolyn Kuebler of *New England Review*; Megan Sexton and Soniah Kamal of *Five Points*; Michael Griffith and Nicola Mason, once again, of *Cincinnati Review*; Jonathan Freedman and Vicki Lawrence of *Michigan Quarterly Review*; Linda Swanson-Davies and Susan Burmeister-Brown of *Glimmer Train*; Stephen Corey of *Georgia Review*; and Bill Henderson of *The Pushcart Prize*.

To the Smittcamp family and all the staff and leaders of the Smittcamp Family Honors College, who have created a miracle and sustain it daily.

To my fellow students from English 42H in fall of 2002.

I am deeply thankful to my parents, Tom Chatagnier and Sylvia Chatagnier. Their support has been constant and multifaceted all the years of my life.

I am deeply grateful for my children, Ishmael and Colette. They have the best hearts of anyone I know.

And above all, I am thankful for Laura, whose love makes the world I live in.

Stories from this volume first appeared, some in altered form, in: *Cincinnati Review* ("The Unplayable Études"), *Five Points* ("Every Face in the Crowd" as "Every Face Was in the Crowd"), *Georgia Review* ("Retrograde Mountain Time"), *Glimmer Train* ("Dentists"), *Kenyon Review Online* ("The Law of Threes"), *Michigan Quarterly Review* ("As Long as the Laughter" as "Warnings from the Future"), *New England Review* and *The Pushcart Prize XLII* ("Miracle Fruit").